Welcome to this month's books from Harlequin Presents! The fabulously passionate series THE ROYAL HOUSE OF NIROLI continues with *The Tycoon's Princess Bride* by Natasha Oakley, where Princess Isabella Fierezza risks forfeiting her chance to be queen when she falls for Niroli's enemy, Domenic Vincini. And don't miss *The Spanish Prince's Virgin Bride*, the final part of Sandra Marton's trilogy THE BILLIONAIRES' BRIDES, in which Prince Lucas Reyes believes his contract fiancée is pretending she's never been touched by another man!

Also this month, favorite author Helen Bianchin brings you *The Greek Tycoon's Virgin Wife*, where gorgeous Xandro Caramanis wants a wife—and an heir. In *Innocent on Her Wedding Night* by Sara Craven, Daniel meets his estranged wife again—and wants to claim the wedding night that was never his. In *The Boss's Wife for a Week* by Anne McAllister, Spence Tyack's assistant Sadie proves not only to be sensible in the boardroom, but also sensual in the bedroom! In *The Mediterranean Billionaire's Secret Baby* by Diana Hamilton, Italian billionaire Francesco Mastroianni is shocked to see his ex-mistress again after seven months—and she's visibly pregnant! In *Willingly Bedded, Forcibly Wedded* by Melanie Milburne, Jasper Caulfield has to marry Hayley or he'll lose his inheritance. But she's determined to be a wife on paper only. Finally brilliant new author India Grey brings you her first book, *The Italian's Defiant Mistress*, where only millionaire Raphael di Lazaro can help Eve—if she becomes his mistress....

Diana Hamilton
THE MEDITERRANEAN BILLIONAIRE'S SECRET BABY

ITALIAN HUSBANDS

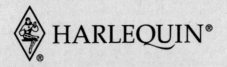

HARLEQUIN®

TORONTO • NEW YORK • LONDON
AMSTERDAM • PARIS • SYDNEY • HAMBURG
STOCKHOLM • ATHENS • TOKYO • MILAN • MADRID
PRAGUE • WARSAW • BUDAPEST • AUCKLAND

ISBN-13: 978-0-373-12672-9
ISBN-10:   0-373-12672-7

THE MEDITERRANEAN BILLIONAIRE'S SECRET BABY

First North American Publication 2007.

Copyright © 2007 by Diana Hamilton.

www.eHarlequin.com

Printed in U.S.A.

All about the author...
Diana Hamilton

DIANA HAMILTON lives with her husband in a beautiful part of Shropshire, in an idyll shared with two young Cavalier King Charles spaniels and a cat named Rackety-Cat. Her three children and their assorted offspring are frequent visitors. When she's not writing for Harlequin Presents, Diana's driving her sports car—and frightening the locals—pottering in the garden, or lazing in the sun beneath a ridiculous hat, reading.

Diana has been fascinated by the written word from an early age and firmly believes she was born with her nose in a book.

After leaving grammar school she studied fine art, but put her real energy into gaining her advertising copywriting degree. She worked as a copywriter until her family moved to a remote part of Wales, where her third child was born. Four years later they returned to Shropshire, where they have been ever since, gradually restoring the rambling Elizabethan manor that Diana gave her heart to on sight. In the mid-seventies Diana took up her pen again. Over the following ten years she wrote thirty novels for Robert Hale of London, while raising her children and continuing restoration work on her home.

In 1987 Diana realized her dearest ambition—the publication of her first Harlequin romance. She had come home. And that warm feeling persists to this day as, more than forty-five Harlequin Presents novels later, she is still in love with the genre.

CHAPTER ONE

DARK brows clenched in irritation above narrowed smoke-grey eyes, Francesco Mastroianni drove through the gathering gloom of a chilly March evening. Vicious rods of rain hit the windscreen of the throatily growling Ferarri, adding to his already sour mood.

Visiting this part of rural Gloucestershire wasn't his idea of a picnic—there were too many uncomfortable memories—but there was no way he could have excused his way out of it. He was too fond of Silvana even to think of turning the weekend invitation down and spoiling her pleasure in showing off her new home.

Trouble was, his cousin Silvana and her husband Guy had recently moved from their swanky London abode to a newly renovated manor house in a county that sent a shiver through him whenever the name was mentioned.

He didn't do cringing, and he found the grossly unwelcome experience infuriating.

Per l'amor del cielo—just get over it! he instructed himself toughly, gritting his teeth until his jaw resembled something carved out of rock. However painful the experience, he'd learned a priceless lesson—hadn't he?

Francesco had been cynical where the female sex was concerned since he'd entered his late teens and learned that his family's wealth was a powerful magnet. It was hard to credit that he'd actually been besotted and bewitched into allowing himself to believe that, against all his previous expectations, he'd finally found one woman he could trust. Actually to believe she was the one woman in the world he could trust with his life and his love until the day he died.

His sweet Anna—his mouth curled with cynical derision.

Yeah. Right.

He'd been well and truly suckered! Behaving like a callow youth instead of a mature and worldly-wise hard-nosed thirty-four-year-old!

She'd turned out to be as bad as all the others who'd targeted his personal fortune—worse, even. Pretending—oh, she'd been good at pretending—that she had no idea who he was, pretending she believed he was just a regular guy, earning a crust whichever way he could by fishing, acting as a part-time tour guide, taking casual work wherever he found it. That was the impression she'd seemingly arrived at, and although he hadn't lied he hadn't disabused her, too delighted to have found himself falling for the beautiful, gentle Anna who, so it had seemed, had been in love with him, the man, not with his financial clout.

Expelling a savage hiss of breath between strong white teeth, he slowed down to a crawl at a fork in the narrow lane and peered out through the murk at the signpost.

Left towards his cousin's new home. Right towards the

village where Anna the sneaky gold-digger lived. Rylands. The name of her home was burned into his brain.

He was powerless to prevent his mind flicking back to the last time he'd made this journey.

'Make your way there—I'll tell my folks to expect you and make a bed up. You will stay overnight, won't you?' She'd sounded breathless with excitement when he'd phoned from London to say he was on his way to see her. 'It's a real pain—but I won't be back until around ten. I'll be working this evening. And, no...' a breathy sigh, a sigh that had seemed to his bamboozled self to hold every last ounce of the world's regrets '...I can't cancel—wish I could! Oh, Francesco, I can't wait to see you!'

Replacing the receiver on one of the bank of phones that sat on the gleaming expanse of his desk in the glass and polished teak office of his London headquarters, he'd grinned wryly. He'd already cancelled three scheduled meetings to be with her. But that wouldn't occur to her. Why should it? She hadn't a clue that he headed the vast Mastroianni business empire that ran like well-oiled clockwork from offices in Rome, Brussels, New York and Sydney.

Buzzing through to his senior PA, he'd imparted the information that he was leaving—with a proposal bursting to trip off his tongue and a ring fit for a queen in the breast pocket of his pale grey business suit—reflecting that, though the delay of a few hours in seeing her was more than he could bear, it would at least give him the opportunity to get to know her parents.

Her father had been waiting to greet him. A large,

florid figure in shabby tweeds, he'd bounded down the short flight of stone steps like a boisterous overgrown puppy, hardly giving him time to take in the proportions of the seventeenth-century building constructed of mellow golden Cotswold stone. Or the general look of dilapidation.

'So you are my little girl's fella!' His hands grasped in a knuckle-crushing grip, he'd watched the older man's eyes widen in recognition and then narrow as he as good as licked his lips. 'Welcome to the ancestral home! Anna's told us all about you!'

Led through a huge stone-flagged hall, empty apart from a solitary sorry-looking chair, he'd found himself ushered into a smallish panelled room cluttered with shabby sofas and a scuffed pine table and treated to the most blatant begging spiel he'd ever had to endure.

'Thought I'd get this in before my good lady joins us— you know how it is; they don't understand business matters, bless their pretty little heads! Thing is, old son, I've got this fantastic idea. Can't lose! Great investment opportunity for a man like you. You'd be a fool to turn it down, and from what I've read about you, you're not that!'

Dismissing the crackpot scheme—something to do with wild animals—he'd felt his heart twist with the shock of betrayal, his face stiffen with anger. So Anna had told her father all about her 'fella'? You bet she had! Got him primed and ready to swoop!

No wonder she'd sounded over the moon when he'd phoned to say he was on his way. Congratulating herself that she'd successfully reeled him in!

Had the working excuse been just that? A lie, giving

her father the time and space to wheedle a million pounds from him? Would his sweet Anna have swanned in when the deal was done and dusted, widening those big green eyes and fluttering those thick lashes, exclaiming with a pout of her luscious lips that she didn't understand boring business stuff, confident that fantastic sex would hold him?

His voice like a razor, he'd cut the older man off midflow. 'I've never been begged for money more clumsily.' Then he'd asked for a sheet of paper. Scrawled a message for his 'Sweet Anna', and left. Despising himself. Hating her.

Hating her for turning him into the sort of fool who could be led from the heart instead of the head.

He who prided himself on his cool, calculating brain, his inborn ability to recognise a gold-digger at a hundred yards, had come within a whisker of being taken for the ride of his life.

He was deeply ashamed of himself.

Gunning the engine, he took the left fork and told himself to forget the whole distasteful episode. And hoped with savage impatience that Silvana—an incorrigible matchmaker—hadn't included a wannabe billionaire's wife/mistress in her weekend invitation. He had no interest in the opposite sex. Hadn't had since—oh, forget it!

Her hands pressing against the aching small of her back, Anna Maybury regarded her feet, shod in comfy old black flatties. She was sure her ankles were swelling. One of the penalties of being seven months pregnant.

Her hands slid round to rest lightly on her bump, which was only partially disguised by her voluminous pale green working overall. Despite the discomfort, she loved her coming baby more than she'd ever thought possible.

A termination, as suggested by a couple of her friends, had been completely out of the question, and her parents' nagging on about her right to contact the father and demand financial support had been met with stubborn refusal.

This was her baby, and she loved him or her with every atom of her generous heart. She would manage without any input from its father. The very idea made her seethe. He was an utter cad! He might be more handsome than was good for any man, and, as it had turned out, filthy rotten rich, but he was still a callous, womanising louse!

Annoyed with herself for giving him space in her head, breaking the staunch vow she'd made never to think of him again, she tucked a straying strand of her mane of long blonde hair back beneath the unflattering snood and gave her attention to the makings of dinner for four. The pre-prepared items were waiting in the cool box, and the leg of lamb spiked with garlic and rosemary, for the main course, was sizzling nicely in the oven of the huge old range.

An Italian menu, as stipulated. Anna didn't want to think of anything Italian. Maybe that was why she'd dropped her mental guard and allowed herself to give her baby's father head-room—something she'd successfully avoided ever since she'd discovered she was pregnant.

Apparently her client, Silvana Rosewall, was Italian,

married to some well-heeled English banker. So she'd have to get herself comfy with that and not give in to self-pity just because the lady of the house had stipulated an Italian menu.

She was a professional chef, and her home catering business was doing OK. More than OK. Though she could have done with her friend Cissie's help tonight, to take over the actual serving.

But Cissie had a promising date, and when she'd first offered to join Maybury Catering in a dogsbody and PR capacity she'd stressed that she would only be filling in time until Mr Right and Rich came over her horizon.

She had to hand it to Cissie, though. Her family had all the right social connections, and a word here and there had produced some good bookings—like tonight's—and they were infinitely preferable to the others that came in—mostly childrens' parties or buffet lunches for leisured ladies—handed to her like patronising favours because people knew her family and were sorry for them.

But she was not, *not* going to think about the very real prospect that Rylands, the family home for over three hundred years, might be taken from them. It was a scary thought, because she knew that losing her family's home would break her mother's already frail heart. And agonising over such scary thoughts would be bad for her unborn baby. So she wouldn't let herself.

'My guests have just arrived.'

A smile lighting her heart-shaped face, Anna turned as Mrs Rosewall entered the huge kitchen. Relief that things would now start moving, occupy a mind that annoyingly seemed inclined to brood, flooded through her. The kitchen was way at the back of the rambling manor, so she hadn't been able to hear car tyres crunching on the gravel of the main driveway.

'What do we have?' Silvana Rosewall picked her way over the uneven slate flooring slabs that had been *in situ* since the house was built. A woman in her early thirties, she was beautiful in a blue silk gown, spiky high heels, with a cluster of jewels somehow fixed in her upswept dark hair.

'Tiny hot potato cakes with mozzarella to start, followed by swordfish kebabs, then thin slices of Tuscan-style lamb, with roasted Mediterranean vegetables, and to finish we have zabaglione with caramel oranges,' Anna reeled off confidently. 'And coffee, of course. And I managed to get hold of some of those special Venetian biscuits.'

'*Excellente.*' Silvana nodded her approval. 'We eat in half an hour.' A slight frown marred the perfection of her smooth-as-cream brow as her eyes swept Anna's dumpily pregnant figure. 'You are alone? You can manage—in your condition? I would have thought some other person to wait on the table…'

Someone slim and attractive, not likely to put her guests off their food, Anna translated wryly as her client finally closed the kitchen door behind her. Well, she'd do her best to melt into the background. She had the sort of curves that would have looked great on a six-foot Amazon, but in her own eyes they made her five-two frame decidedly dumpy. Normally she was saved from complete rotundity only by her once tiny waist—although recently that had ballooned with her large and growing larger vigorous baby!

Dismissing her apple-like shape, Anna opened the first of the two large cool boxes which held everything that could have possibly been prepared at home and got on with what she did best. Cooking.

Exactly half an hour later the biggest tray she could find was loaded with four plates of sizzling hot potato cakes topped with melting, slightly browned mozzarella and garnished with fresh basil, and she was on her way, her heart light because all was going as it should. The lamb was resting now, before carving, and the swordfish, tomato and lemon wedge kebabs were ready to put under the grill the moment she was back in the kitchen after unobtrusively serving the *antipasto*. Hopefully the Rosewalls and their two guests would be so knocked out by the delicious food she was serving they wouldn't notice her, and her appearance wouldn't be an embarrassment to her fastidious client.

But her blithe confidence took a shattering nosedive when she entered the panelled room and stared straight into the eyes of…him!

The loaded tray almost followed the abrupt direction of her confidence. Clinging to it for dear life, she felt her face flame. His eyes impaled her. The last time she'd looked into them they'd glimmered between the unfairly long and thick sweep of his dark lashes, smoky with desire. Now they were hard, glitteringly dark and dangerously narrowed.

Gunfighter's eyes, she thought crazily, and swallowed down a cry of outrage. She dropped her transfixed gaze, willed the fiery colour to leave her hot face, and handed the plates around, her hands shaking.

Scuttling out of the room, her dignity long-lost, she made it back to the kitchen. Her heart pounding, Anna leant back against the solid wood of the closed door and tried to pull herself together. Seeing him here—smooth, urbanely handsome, in the sort of beautifully tailored suit that must have cost an arm and a leg, looking at her as if she were something quite unspeakable—had been a cruel shock.

The taunting words he'd scrawled on that note he'd left for her were etched in acid behind her closed eyes.

Nice try. But I've changed my mind. You've a lot to offer, but nothing I can't get in spades elsewhere.

Sex. He'd meant sex.

Her stomach lurched and she thrust a fisted hand against her mouth. Dad must have read the note. Nothing else could have explained his hangdog expression when he'd handed it to her, mumbling that her new fella had only stayed for ten minutes, then left. So her father knew she'd been given the runaround, and that had made her feel even worse, if that were possible.

At first she'd thought that he'd believed she was loaded—hadn't she and Cissie been staying at that ruinously expensive hotel, patronised by the seriously wealthy? He'd thought he was onto a good thing—until he'd faced the reality of Rylands, denuded of anything worth selling, neglect evident everywhere you looked.

That had been before. A few weeks later Cissie had thrust one of the glossy society magazines her mother took under her nose, a scarlet nail jabbing at a photograph.

'That's the guy you hooked up with on Ischia. I thought he looked sort of familiar, but I couldn't place him—it must have been the scruff he was going around in. He must have been incognito—not a minder or a fancy yacht in sight! He's always in the gossip columns of the glossies. He's worth trillions—you lucky cow! Do you keep in touch?'

'No.'

'Pity. Hook him and you'd be set for life! Mind you, to be honest, these holiday flings aren't meant to last, and I guess he'd be a handful—terrible reputation with women!'

Shrugging, she'd turned away, barely glancing at the photographed Francesco Mastroianni, his white dinner jacket contrasting with his fatally attractive dark Latin looks, complete with arm candy. Her mind had felt fried. He hadn't been after her non-existent family money, as she'd first thought.

Just sex.

But in the short time between arriving in London and phoning her he'd met someone who could give him better sex—someone more sophisticated. Creep! Oh, how she hated men who used women as playthings, to be picked up and then chucked away when a more exciting prospect came into view!

So what right had he to look at her now as if she were beneath contempt?

Heaving herself away from the door, she told herself that if anyone deserved contempt it was him, and rushed to turn on the grill.

She was a professional. She would do the job she'd been hired to do, ignore him and, when the evening was over, she'd put him right out of her head again. She would not, *not* 'accidentally' knock his wine glass over into his lap, or drop a loaded plate on his hateful head. She couldn't afford that sort of satisfaction. To get a reputation for gross clumsiness would mean she'd never work in the area again.

But if he dared give her that contemptuous look one more time she'd be sorely tempted!

She was pregnant!

His?

Francesco had to force himself to eat. Force himself to ignore Anna Maybury as she served them. Force out the occasional monosyllable that was his sole contribution to the otherwise animated conversation, oblivious to the come-ons that were steaming his way from the sultry redhead his cousin had produced for his delectation.

Not interested. Not remotely. Grimly sifting facts.

Anna had been a virgin. He hadn't used protection that first time, too blown away to even think of it.

Lost. He'd been lost in a wildly churning maelstrom of unfettered emotion—an experience so new and vivid he'd felt as if the whole of his life up until that moment had been a theatre of shadows.

The child she was carrying could be his. Unless—

Aiming for casual, he leaned back, hooked an arm over the back of his chair and, ignoring the redhead's pouting smile, tossed into the conversation, 'Your caterer? How pregnant is she, do you know?'

Three pairs of taken-aback eyes stared at him. It was Silvana who wanted to know, 'Why do you ask?'

Because I might be about to be a father and not know it. Aloud, he responded with deceptive idleness. 'I wondered if we, collectively, might be required to act as midwives.'

An irritating tinkle of laughter from the redhead—he couldn't remember what she was called—and an apprehensive glance from Guy towards his wife, who answered. 'Seven months, according to Cissie Lansdale. Cissie's a sort of partner on Anna's catering business— a bit feckless, I think the word is. She usually helps out with the waiting—but not tonight, apparently. Guy, darling—our glasses are empty.'

As her husband did the honours with a second bottle of Valpolicella, Silvana confided, 'Personally, I think a woman in her position should be resting, not—' she waved a languid hand over the table '—doing this sort of thing. Of course she doesn't have a husband to lay the law down, and her mother's a feeble thing—not in good health, I hear. Besides, I suppose they need the money. The father's hopeless. He married into that family. They once had real standing in the area. But he squandered everything or lost it.'

'Bad investments followed worse ones, I hear,' Guy put in as he sat down again.

'You seem to know a lot about them,' Francesco commented, reflecting uneasily that seven months was spot-on. The child would be his unless immediately on her return home Anna had jumped into bed with someone else. But that didn't seem likely, given that at that time she'd been banking on reeling him in. She'd been expecting him to follow her to England, so she would not have wanted some other guy hanging around to stir up trouble, he decided forensically.

Making a huge effort to stop a black scowl from forming, and stopping himself from marching straight into the kitchen and demanding to know the truth, he listened to his cousin's answer.

'It was necessary when we first came here to introduce ourselves to the better families so they could advise us on local reliable and honest tradespeople. A permanent housekeeper is to arrive next week, but there are others.' She took a sip of her coffee and arched one finely raised brow at him over the central flower arrangement. 'Plumbers, electricians, a man to do the garden, caterers—that sort of person. The pregnant girl came highly recommended.

'Now, why don't we retire to the sitting room while the pregnant one clears away? One Grappa, I think, and then Guy and I will go up and leave you two to relax by the fire and get to know each other properly.' A big smile in Francesco's direction as she got to her feet. 'I know Natalie wants to discuss some charity ball I'm sure you'll be interested in.'

Like hell he would! Deadpan, he met the redhead's over-sugared smile. Introduced by Silvana as 'a friend from London'—an organiser of glittering events for some charity or other—she was certainly a looker. And available. And he was going to have to endure a weekend of having his cousin throwing them together. He would have to let this Natalie know that he was as interested in the female of the species as he was in settling down to read through the telephone directory from cover to cover. And try to be kind about it.

And tomorrow, first thing, he would visit Rylands and demand to know if the child the woman who'd made an idiot of him was carrying was his.

The dishwasher had finished its cycle. Wearily, Anna replaced the contents back in place in the huge Victorian floor-to-ceiling cupboard. Her feet were burning and her back was still aching.

Half an hour earlier Mrs Rosewall had found her re-packing the cool boxes and handed her a cheque.

'The meal was perfect. Are you almost finished?'

'Everything will be back as it was in half an hour or so. I'm just waiting for the dishes to finish. Unless you'd prefer me to leave now?' Said without any real hope.

She'd been longing to get away—well out of the orbit of Francesco and his current woman. But from experience she knew that her clients wanted their kitchens to look as if they'd never been used. That was what they paid her for. And they wanted full value for money.

And this one was no different. 'No hurry. I just wanted to tell you that my husband and I are retiring for the night, but my cousin and his young lady will be in the sitting room and I don't want them to be disturbed. Just let yourself out quietly. And, while I think about it, could you cater for lunch on Sunday? My guests will be driving back to London in the afternoon, so nothing too heavy, I think.'

Anna hadn't even considered saying yes! The fee would be more than welcome, but no way would she put herself anywhere near that womanising creep again!

'Sorry,' she'd declined, resisting the urge to rub her aching back. 'That won't be possible.'

Now, after a final look at the spotless kitchen, she got into her old raincoat, shook her hair free and let herself out. Too tired to hurry, she was drenched when she reached her van and loaded the cool boxes in the back.

It had been a nightmare of a night. The shock of seeing him again had got to her, brought it all back when she hadn't wanted to so much as think about him again. But it was over now, she reminded herself with almost tearful gratitude, and she forced herself to look on the bright side.

Sensibly telling herself that she never need set eyes on him again, she clambered in behind the wheel.

The way that redhead had been positively drooling over him had made her feel nauseous, and the horrible feeling that he must have noticed her pregnant state—how could he miss it?—put two and two together and know that the baby was his had been argued away as she'd grilled the kebabs.

Callously, he wouldn't want to know. What had happened on Ischia was just one in a long line of forgettable flings. He would dismiss the matter, reasoning that if she had fallen pregnant it was her own fault and she could deal with it.

Which was fine by her!

With his heart successfully painted as black as his midnight hair, Anna pushed him roughly out of her mind and turned the key in the ignition.

The engine gave a tortured whine—and died. After the fourth attempt Anna had to concede that the battery was dead. Sternly resisting the temptation to bawl her eyes out, she rooted in her handbag for her mobile. It was entirely her own fault. Nick had advised her to splash out on a new battery, but she had kept putting it off because every spare penny was needed to pay the service bills at Rylands and put food on the table.

The fruitless search for her mobile continued—until Anna had to concede that she must have left it at home. Banging her small fists against the steering wheel, she yelped 'Stupid! *Stupid!*' then slumped in exhaustion in her seat, facing the unpalatable fact that she would have to go and knock them up.

'Them' being Francesco and his current squeeze! The Rosewalls had long since retired for the night. And for all she knew so had Francesco and his lady. The thought galvanised her. It had to be all of eight miles back to Rylands. It was pouring with rain. If she weren't pregnant she would walk it. But as it was—

Francesco permitted himself a small Grappa as the redhead vacated the room. Huffily.

Too edgy to settle, he paced the room, glass held loosely in one hand. Used to fending women off, he usually managed it with finesse. Not tonight. He hadn't been brutal. Just cold, clipped, concise.

Tickets for the charity ball she was organising didn't interest him. Neither did meeting up for lunch when they were back in town. His schedule was too tight to allow room for any socialising in the foreseeable future.

At which point she'd gone to bed. Alone.

So he should be able to relax. But he couldn't. Seeing Anna Maybury again had rekindled all the shaming memories, had brought everything he was doing his damnedest to forget back into unbelievably sharp focus, and her advanced state of pregnancy had deeply unsettled him, raising questions he knew he had to have answered.

The morning, when he could confront her, seemed an unendurably long way away.

Her heart quailing, Anna pressed the doorbell. The rain had turned her hair into dripping rats' tails, and the front of her overall was soaking because the bump meant she couldn't fasten her old waterproof. She felt sick with nerves, and knowing she must look pretty dreadful didn't help.

But she had to contact Nick—ask him to come and collect her—and that meant facing Francesco, speaking to him, asking for the use of the Rosewalls' phone.

The alternative was trudging home along narrow, isolated lanes. The chance of flagging down a passing motorist was a remote one at this time of night, and the likelihood of seeing a light at the windows of one of the scattered cottages or farmsteads was almost non-existent.

As the door swung open in answer to her summons at last she stiffened her spine, barely glanced at Francesco's hard, handsome features and managed to get out, in a disgracefully wobbly voice, 'My van won't start. May I use the phone?'

Silence. Then, above the relentless sound of the rain, she heard his harsh indrawn breath, found her eyes tugged up to his. Hardened grey steel.

And not even the beguiling accent could soften the impact of his rawly savage question. 'Tell the truth, for once in your life. Is the baby mine?'

CHAPTER TWO

FLOUNDERING, stunned by such an in-your-face enquiry, Anna decided that it would be more dignified to ignore the question rather than give in to the compulsion to fling *What do you care?* at him.

Woodenly, she elaborated on her request, hammering home the fact that a way out of her present dead van difficulty need be the only point of contact between them.

'I need to call Nick to ask him to fetch me, and for that I obviously need to use a phone.'

Aware of steel-hard eyes boring into her, one sable brow elevated in what looked like disbelief, she squirmed inside. Was he asking himself how he had ever managed to make love—amendment, have sex—with such a creature? Lumpen, hair like wet string, clumpy shoes, old school mac out of which loomed a stomach as big as the Millennium Dome!

Fighting the appalling fizzy upsurge of hysteria, she forced herself to calm down, to forget she loathed and despised him, and to explain, slowly and clearly, flattening dangerous emotions out of her voice. 'Please let the Rosewalls know that Nick and I will collect my van first thing in the morning. All it needs is a new battery.' Fingers crossed! No way could she pay a big repair bill if there was anything more serious amiss.

Shivering now, wet, cold and intensely weary, she felt desperation claw at her as she took a step forward. 'May I come in?'

Glancing up at him when he made no move to allow her entry, she felt her heart twist in alarm. His eyes were grim and his beautiful, sexy mouth was set in a cruel slash. The handsome features were taut, throwing those classical cheekbones and the arrogant blade of his nose into harsh relief.

Was he going to tell her to get lost? Force her to walk back?

He moved then. Towards her. Taking an elbow in a grip of steel, turning her. 'I'll drive you.'

'That's not necessary.' She couldn't hide the note of urgency in her voice, dreading the thought of being cooped up in a car with him, him repeating That Question, getting personal. 'Nick will be more than happy to fetch me.'

His grip tightened. The pace he was setting as he steered her unwilling and yet too exhausted to fight self through the darkness to the far side of the manor house quickened. 'I'm sure he will,' he remarked sardonically. 'However, you need to get out of those wet things and into a hot bath as quickly as possible.' He tugged her to a halt before she could blunder into the parked Ferrari. 'You do not have just your own well-being to consider now.'

He meant the baby, Anna conceded guiltily as she shoehorned herself into the passenger seat. And he was right. The whole evening had been disastrous, and she needed to get dry, warm and relaxed for her baby's sake, but the comparative speed of that operation against the delay of waiting for Nick meant Francesco would have ample opportunity to ask That Question again, and she didn't know how to answer him.

Her spine rigid with apprehension, she felt hot tears of sheer exhaustion flood her eyes, and she bit into the soft underside of her lower lip to stop them falling.

Tell him it was none of his business? Would he accept that? Absent himself smartly, relieved that she wouldn't be making a nuisance of herself, demanding financial support, and—heaven forbid—making herself known to his family and causing him huge embarrassment?

It seemed a definite possibility. As a psychological profile of a guy who would trample a poor girl's heart with as much compunction as he would trample a fallen leaf, it fitted.

Unless she steeled herself to tell a whopping lie and name some other fictional guy as the father? Claim she was just five months pregnant, putting him right out of the frame? But, given the size of her, would he be gormless enough to believe that?

Bracing herself, Anna waited. But the only question he asked was, 'Do you still live with your parents at Rylands?' Receiving a breathless affirmative, he said nothing more until he halted the car at the head of the weedy drive. Then he told her grimly, 'Don't think I've finished. I'll be here first thing in the morning. And if I'm told you're not available I'll wait until you are.'

* * *

Driving back at the sort of speed he had earlier carefully controlled in deference to his passenger, Francesco cursed himself for failing to demand to know the identity of the father of her child.

Once set on a course of action he always pursued it with surgical precision, letting nothing stand in his way. He was single-minded, known to be ruthless when the occasion demanded—he'd had to be. Taking over the almost moribund Mastroianni business empire on the death of his father ten years earlier, he'd dragged it kicking and screaming, into the twenty-first century—not a task for an indecisive weakling.

And as for compassion for fools and knaves—forget it!

So why hadn't he pressed home his advantage when she'd asked to use the Rosewalls' phone? Why had he allowed her to avoid answering the burning question? No one else on the planet would have got away with it!

He should have forced the truth from her. He'd had the ideal opportunity.

Except—

She'd looked so vulnerable. Exhausted. Wet and bed-raggled, like a half-drowned kitten. His primary emotion had been rage that a woman in her condition was forced to slave for those too privileged to do anything but issue orders and then sit back and wait for them to be carried out. That had been swiftly followed by the need to transport her to where she could find comfort and rest.

He expelled a harsh breath through his teeth. He had to be getting old, losing his touch!

And who the hell was Nick?

* * *

Clutching her hot water bottle, Anna crawled into bed. The bathwater had been tepid at best and her bedroom was draughty, with damp patches on the ceiling where the venerable roof leaked.

Her throat tightened. She shivered convulsively. She was being threatened. He really did mean to drag the truth from her, against all her earlier expectations he wasn't going to shrug those magnificent, expensively clothed shoulders, discount the fact that he might be about to become a father and leave her to get on with it.

She'd read somewhere that the Latin male was deeply family orientated. The reminder made her shudder.

If only she hadn't accepted the Rosewalls' catering job! They wouldn't have set eyes on each other again. And if only she'd been able to fall in love with Nick and accept the offer of marriage that had been made when her pregnancy had begun to show she'd have been a married woman, and Nick would have sworn blind the child was his. He would do anything for her. The thought depressed her.

She and Nick had been best mates since they were toddlers, and he was the kindest, gentlest person she knew. They were deeply fond of each other—always had been—and that had prompted his proposal, and the vow to care for her and the baby, look on him or her as his own.

He cared for her—she knew that—but he was not in love with her and he deserved better. One day he would meet someone who took his breath away. And she wasn't in love with him either. What she felt for Nick was nothing like what she'd felt when she'd fallen for Francesco—

Oh! Scrub that! Punching the pillow with small, angry fists, she buried her head in it and tried to sleep.

Anna gladly left her rumpled bed at daybreak. Dressing in a fresh maternity smock, she bunched up her hair and pinned it on top of her head. Her eyes looked huge and haunted as they stared back at her from the mirror.

Turning away, disgusted with herself for being scared of the Italian Louse, because he couldn't make her do anything she didn't want to do, she stuffed her feet into a pair of beat-up old running shoes. The comfy flats she'd worn last night were still sodden.

She hunted for her mobile.

Nick sounded sleepy when he answered, and Anna apologised. 'I woke you. Oh, I'm sorry! But listen—'

Briefly she explained what she needed, feeling awful for calling him so early. But Francesco hadn't specified a time—just 'first thing'—and if she and Nick were on their way to the manor with a new battery when Francesco turned up, tough. He would have to kick his heels until she decided to return home. And it wouldn't be running away, she assured herself staunchly. No. It would simply be giving her the upper hand.

'No probs,' Nick was saying. 'Give me half an hour. Didn't I tell you you'd get trouble? How did you get home? You should have called me.'

'I was going to. But one of the Rosewalls' guests insisted on driving me.' She skated over that bit quickly. 'And Nick—thanks.'

'What for?'

'Thanks for coming to the rescue.'

'Any time—you know that. Or should do.'

Ending the call, Anna plodded down to the kitchen, collecting her old waxed jacket on the way. A swift glass of juice, and then she'd set out to meet Nick. Thankfully, last night's rain had stopped, and fitful sunlight illuminated the dire shabbiness of the interior.

No wonder poor old Mum seemed to be permanently depressed as she watched her beloved old family home start on the unstoppable slide into decay. Frustrated too. Beatrice Maybury had always been frail—something to do with having had rheumatic fever as a child—and was unable to do anything practical to change the situation. She'd had to stand by and watch her husband William lose everything through one sure-fire money-making scheme after another, all predictably and disastrously failing.

Sighing, she pushed open the door to the cavernous kitchen—and stopped in her tracks.

'Mum?'

Beatrice Maybury, her slight body encased in an ancient candlewick dressing gown, greying hair braided into a single plait that almost reached her waist, her feet stuffed into rubber boots, lifted the kettle from the hotplate and advanced towards the teapot. 'Tea, dear?'

'You're up early.' She watched, green eyes narrowed, as her mother reached another mug from the dresser. Mum rarely surfaced before ten, on her husband's insistence that she rest. William had always treated his adored wife as if she were made of spun glass. It was a pity, Anna thought in a moment of rare sourness, that he hadn't treated the fortune she'd inherited the same way. 'Is anything wrong?'

'No more than usual.' Beatrice's eyes were red-rimmed and watery in the pallor of her face, her smile small and tired as she put two mugs of steaming tea on the table. 'Your father's worn out. I think that job's too much for him. I insisted he had a little lie-in.'

She sat, cradling her mug in her thin hands. Swallowing a sigh, Anna followed suit, beyond hope now of setting out to meet Nick on his way here and thereby avoiding The Louse if he had literally meant 'first thing'. She couldn't just walk out and leave Mum—not while she was so obviously troubled. As far as Anna could remember her mother had never insisted on anything, meekly allowing others to make all decisions, content to follow, never to lead.

Dad had always been as strong as an ox, but maybe labouring for a firm of local builders was proving to be too much for a man well into his sixties. The wages he earned went to make a token payment to his creditors, while the money she earned paid the household bills— just about. Between them they kept Rylands itself in a type of precarious safety. For the moment.

'I said I'd feed Hetty and Horace and let them out. No egg this morning. I think Hetty's off-colour.'

Anna grinned. It was the first time she'd felt remotely like smiling since she'd clapped eyes on The Louse again. 'She's probably just miffed because you keep taking her eggs. We should let her sit, increase the flock.'

The cockerel and the fat brown hen were the only survivors of a fox raid—the only survivors of Dad's self-sufficiency drive. It had been announced with his unending brio, hazel eyes alight with this new enthusiasm, grin as wide as a barn door. 'Fruit and veg, hens, a pig, a goat. The lot. Keep ourselves like royalty; sell the surplus in the village. Goat cheese, bacon, free-range eggs—you name it! Forget big business—back to nature. That's the life for us!'

The goat had never materialised. The pig had died. A neighbouring farmer's sheep had got in and trampled or eaten the fruit and veg, and the fox had taken the hens.

'And...' Beatrice raised soft blue eyes to her daughter, 'We had a little tiff. He was upset, I'm afraid.'

Anna put her mug down on the pitted table-top. She didn't like the sound of this. Her parents doted on each other. The love they shared was the staunch prop that kept their lives from collapsing around them, becoming a bitter nightmare. Mum had never said a cross word, had never blamed Dad when his bad investments and wacky money-making schemes had gone belly-up. She blamed everyone else instead, always encouraging him in his next, ill-fated 'Big Idea'.

If they were starting to fight, if love and loyalty were slipping away, then what hope was there for them?

Anna loved them both dearly. She felt protective towards her frail mother, and was exasperated by her father, but she loved him for his boundless energy and enthusiasm, his warmth and gruff kindness.

'Well, I'm afraid I'm going to have to put my foot down. Rather firmly.'

'I see,' Anna said gently, astonished by this departure from the norm. But she didn't. 'About...?'

She wasn't going to get an answer, because the clangs of the great doorbell reverberated through the house. She rose. 'That will be Nick. Look, I'm sorry, but I have to go. We'll talk later.' Grabbing her old waxed jacket, wriggling into it, she added automatically, 'Make sure you have breakfast. There's enough bread for toast. I'll pick up another loaf on my way back.'

A detour to the village to pick up a few essential provisions once the new battery was fitted would do nicely. She meant to avoid Francesco Mastroianni for as long as she possibly could, placing herself in a controlling position, hoping she'd be better able to handle the interrogation he obviously intended. Provided, of course, that he didn't emerge from the manor and catch them mid-operation. The thought made her feel vaguely sick as she opened the main door to admit a blast of chilly morning air.

And him.

Francesco swept inside, past her stunned personage. Her tummy flipped. Why did he have to be up and about so early? Couldn't his latest luscious bedmate have kept him glued to her for longer? And this morning he was looking quite unreasonably spectacular.

Six foot two of dominating Italian masculinity—midnight hair superbly styled, midnight lashes narrowed over glinting steel-grey eyes, handsome mouth a sardonic twist as he remarked, 'Going somewhere?'

To her great annoyance Anna felt her face grow hot and pink. To think she had once believed herself fathoms-deep in love with this domineering, sarcastic brute! He'd expertly hidden that side of him from her when he'd set out to seduce her. And dump her.

The immaculately crafted pale grey designer suit emphasised his fantastic physique, his classical features.

The crisp white shirt darkened the tones of his olive skin and the shadowed jawline that remained just that, no matter how often he shaved.

He was an intimidating stranger.

On the island he'd always worn old cut-off denims, canvas deck shoes that had seen better days, and round his neck a fake gold chain that had left green marks on the sleek bronzed skin of his magnificent torso. Those tell-tale stains had made her heart clench with aching tenderness, had made her love him all the more.

Now she didn't love him at all.

She loathed him, and all he stood for.

And she most certainly wasn't about to give him an answer, open the way for any conversation. Leaving the main door open, she sent up a swift and fervent prayer for Nick's speedy arrival and her consequent escape.

'Is there somewhere more comfortable where we can talk?' His tone told her he was running out of patience, and the unnerving steely scrutiny he was subjecting her to told her he didn't like what he saw.

A shabby nobody who might or might not be carrying his child.

'No.' She didn't want to discuss her baby's paternity with him. With anyone. And because she already loved her coming child with all her generous heart she was deeply afraid.

If Francesco knew he was the father he might be more than happy to wash his hands of the whole thing— dismiss it with a shrug. Or—and this was what made her nerves jump—he might come over all macho, wealthy Italian male and demand custody.

And then what would she do? Could she fight him through the courts and win?

'Anna—who is it?' Beatrice appeared from the kitchen region. She stopped dead, clutching the neckline of her shabby robe to her throat. 'I heard voices. It didn't sound like Nick.'

Well, it wouldn't, would it? No one could mistake Francesco's deep, cultured and slightly accented voice for Nick's comforting country burr, Anna thought wearily, wishing her mother had stayed firmly where she was. How was she supposed to introduce him? By the way—this is the man who seduced me, lied to me and dumped me!

It was Francesco who took over, his compressed lips softening into a staggeringly devastating smile as he advanced towards the older woman, his bronzed and far too handsome features relaxing.

'Mrs Maybury. I'm so happy to meet Anna's mother.' He held out a well-shaped hand. After a moment's hesitation, and a swift look at her daughter, Beatrice took it, and went bright pink when it was lifted to the stranger's lips.

'Anna?'

'Francesco Mastroianni,' Anna introduced stiffly. She wanted to shake her mother for simpering and fluttering like a silly schoolgirl, but resignedly forgave her—because no woman alive would be able to stay sensible when bombarded by the charm he could turn on at will when it suited him.

'I met Anna again last night when she catered for my cousin's dinner party,' he was saying. 'I am now here to enquire as to her health.'

Like hell you are! she fumed inwardly, hating him for

his ability to lie and deceive, for looking so sensational, so poised and self-assured, and loathing him for her own helplessness to do anything about it.

Mum had obviously picked up on that word *again*, judging from the way she arched a brow and gave a little moue of a smile. Then, 'How kind of you, *signor*. Won't you come through to the kitchen? It's the only warm room in the house, I'm afraid. And, darling, do close the door. Such a draught!'

Lumbering over the vast expanse of empty hall, Anna was fuming. Mum wouldn't let him over the threshold if she knew the truth. Underneath that fantastic exterior lurked a black devil—a heartless deceiver who would seduce a virgin, tell her he loved her more than his life, ensuring a more than willing bedmate for a couple of weeks to satisfy his massive male libido, his huge conceit, then callously dump her when a new and better prospect shashayed over the horizon.

Preoccupied, it took her several seconds to register that Nick was walking in through the wide open doorway. With his cheerful open face, his mop of untidy nut-brown hair and mild blue eyes, his sturdy body clad in oil-stained jeans and an ancient fleece, he looked so safe and ordinary she could have wept.

'Ready?' His smile encompassed Beatrice. 'Hi, Mrs Maybury!' If he had registered the presence of the superbly groomed stranger he didn't show it. 'Got the van keys?' Assimilating Anna's edgy nod, he supplied, 'Then we'll make tracks. Dad said no need to rush to pay for the battery. It'll wait until it's convenient.'

Anna ground her teeth and felt heated colour flood

her face. Nick's father owned the village garage and he, like everyone else around here, knew of their dire financial situation. His offer of deferred payment was a kind one, but she wished it hadn't been voiced in front of Francesco. She did have *some* pride!

'That won't be necessary,' she put in stiffly, heading for the door, the back of her neck prickling in her need to put as much distance as possible between herself and Francesco whose very presence affected her like an arrow to her heart.

An imperiously drawled, 'Wait!' stopped her.

Exuding sophisticated cool, Francesco stepped forward. 'Nick? I take it you are he?' Receiving a startled glance that he took as an affirmative, he ordered with the sublime confidence of a man who expected to be unquestioningly obeyed, 'There's no need for you to wait. Fix the battery. I'll take Anna to collect her van later.'

'Now, hang on a minute!' Incensed by his assumption that he could call the shots, Anna swung round to face him—and then wished she hadn't. Because just looking at him, at the upward drift of one strongly marked sable brow, the slight querying smile on that wide sensual mouth as he waited for her to expand on her explosive objection, made her heart leap, her mouth feel as parched as desert sand, her pulses race as she remembered—

Smothering a groan, feeling the fight ebbing out of her like water down a drain, she capitulated.

Pointless to avoid the interrogation any longer. The longer she spent dodging That Question, the more uptight and jittery she would become. It couldn't be good for her baby.

Flinging Nick an apologetic smile, she said dully, 'Thanks, pal. I'll see you later. There's stuff I've got to talk over with—him.' And if that sounded rude or ungracious, tough.

She didn't feel even remotely gracious as Francesco ushered her in her mother's wake as the older woman headed back to the kitchen. Just sick to her stomach.

CHAPTER THREE

'I REALLY must go and dress properly. What can you be thinking of me?' Beatrice fluttered as she held the door open for them to pass through and tried to hide her ungainly rubber boots beneath the hem of her dressing gown at the same time—a feat which required considerable contortion. With a sideways curious glance at Francesco's darkly handsome, smoothly polished yet formidable bearing, she added on a breathy rush, 'I won't be a moment, and in the meanwhile—Anna, do offer your guest coffee.'

She did no such thing, forcing herself to stand her ground and not be intimidated by her unwelcome guest's aura of remote and chilling dislike.

So he was appalled by the thought that he might have fathered a child on a nobody who came from a family that was seriously down on its uppers? A nobody who was OK for a brief, easily forgotten holiday fling, but as for anything more meaningful or long term—definitely not.

'Well?' Anna sliced into the stinging silence. She lifted her chin to a proud angle, then winced as her baby gave her a hefty kick to remind her of its sturdy existence. Hopefully her unborn child wasn't picking up on the bad vibes between its parents, she thought worriedly.

Automatically she laid a reassuring hand on the mound of her distended stomach—a gesture which Francesco followed with glittering grey eyes.

'I think you know the answer to that,' he stated, his smooth-as-rich-chocolate voice edged with the harshness of acid. 'And before you tell me whether or not I am the father of your child, be warned. The truthfulness of your answer can be verified, or not, by a simple DNA test.'

He meant it, too! Her half-formed plan to name some fictitious guy and then wait for him to accept it with thankfulness and make a smart exit from her life bit the dust.

As that uncomfortable fact sank in, every scrap of colour leached from her face, leaving her features pinched and her deep green eyes enormous. Since his callous betrayal it had been a relatively simple matter to thrust him out of her head and keep him out, using all her will-power and her instinctive need to protect herself and her precious baby from hurt.

But seeing him again, up close and personal—and what could be more personal than making a baby between them?—was doing terrible things to her emotional equilibrium. Swaying on legs that were no longer strong enough to hold her upright, she pressed her fingertips to suddenly aching temples.

At the speed of a jet plane in a hurry two strong hands were steadying her, easing her down on to a hard kitchen chair.

His starkly explosive expletive brought colour back

to her face as he straightened and stood back a pace, his feet planted apart, his fists bunched into the pockets of his beautifully tailored trousers. Towering above her, he looked darkly menacing, impatience stamped onto each impressive feature.

Stiffening her spine, and dredging up the resolve that had served her so well in the past, refusing to be intimidated, Anna clipped, 'There's no need to swear! And, since you ask—yes, you are the father. You were the first and the last!' She huffed in a deep breath, furious with herself for ever fancying herself in love with such a callous, arrogant creature.

He had the information he had come for now. No way was she going to wait and see which way he ran with it. She said firmly, 'Just understand this: I want nothing from you. Ever. No one will ever hear of your relationship to my baby from me. So you might as well go back to your latest squeeze right now!'

Stark silence greeted her outburst. The strong features were taut, pallor showing beneath the warm olive tones of his skin. Anna tried to guess what he was thinking and couldn't even begin to.

'That is the truth?' Narrowed, penetrating eyes received her mute nod of confirmation and Francesco turned, paced over the uneven flags to stare out of the dingy window.

His child. Flesh of his flesh! His heart clenched.

Dark eyes blazed. His child! Sired on a woman as sneaky as a feral cat. Playing the part of a wide-eyed innocent, pretending she didn't know who he was, enchanting him. And all the while plotting and scheming.

Cleverly manipulating a hardened cynic into the sort of lovelorn idiot that a male over the age of fifteen had no right to be!

And priming her ham-fisted father. How else would he have known that a mere million was peanuts to the man his daughter had ensnared, his for the asking?

Her one mistake.

Besotted, he'd been on the point of asking her to be his wife, offering a lifetime of devoted commitment— something he'd set his face against since he'd been in his late teens. Had she told her father to keep his greedy mouth shut, have patience, then, still besotted, he would have married her, showered gifts on her, secured her family's financial future and lived to bitterly regret it once the scales—as they inevitably would have done— had fallen from his eyes and he'd seen the woman he'd believed to be the love of his life for what she really was.

And as for that vehement statement that she wanted nothing from him—he'd sooner believe the moon was made of cheese! Wait until the child was born, and she'd be there with her demands.

At the sound of the door opening Francesco swung round, his mind assessing the problem he faced like a well-oiled machine, emotions relegated to the area of his brain labelled 'non-productive', fit only to be ignored.

'*Signora.*' Beatrice Maybury's slight frame sported a shabby tweed skirt and a twinset of indeterminate colour. Her long plait was wrapped around her head like a coronet. 'Is your husband in? I would like to speak to you both.' And get this mess sorted out once and for all. No arguments.

'I—' About to chide her daughter for her uncharacteristic lack of manners—for just sitting there like a
block of stone, not providing coffee for her guest or
even asking him to sit, by the look of it—she changed
her mind. Recognising authority, troubled by the sudden
and unwelcome feeling that yet another catastrophe was
about to descend on her weary head, she nodded in mute
obedience and fled.

'There's no need to drag my parents into this.' Anna,
petrified by his now brooding silence, was stung into
speech. 'They don't know you from Adam.'

'I have met your father,' Francesco countered on a
splintered bite. 'Remember?'

How could she forget? He'd dropped by, stayed long
enough to scribble that Dear John note, and left to take
up a more exciting project. 'I'm surprised you reminded
me!' she uttered furiously, scornful of the arrogance of
a man who could calmly introduce the subject of his bad
behaviour without turning a hair.

Some of her abundant crinkly hair had fallen down
into her eyes. She swiped it away and stated, 'I'm trying
to explain—if you'll shut up and listen—that they don't
know who the father of my child is. Nobody does. And
as that's the way it's going to stay, you might as well
leave right now!' she tacked on, incensed by the way he
was looking at her—as if she were a boring child having
a tedious tantrum.

Fully expecting him to swing on the heels of his
handmade shoes and make a swift exit, after yet another
deliberately inelegant slice of rudeness, Anna sagged
back against the chair, feeling dizzy and drained, sting-

ingly aware of the spectacular, darkly narrowed eyes that never left her.

'Just go,' she uttered tiredly—and too late, because her father had made an entrance. Or rather, she amended, crept in, closely followed by her anxious-looking mother.

'Well—this is a surprise!' Two paces into the room and her father had pulled himself together, Anna noted. He was trying to smile now, rubbing his big, work-coarsened hands together in a show of bonhomie.

Only a show, though. She could detect apprehension in his eyes, discomfort in that smile. Sympathising, she put it down to understandable bewilderment following on from that first meeting, when this Italian had breezed in and handed him a note to pass on to his daughter, all those months ago.

'We'll sit.'

Typical! Anna fumed. He Who Must Be Obeyed had spoken! Francesco was taking charge, as if they were in his home, not he the uninvited and as far as she was concerned unwanted guest in theirs—as if they were a clutch of dim-witted underlings about to receive a right royal dressing-down.

It annoyed her to see Dad meekly comply, his head bowed, while Mum dithered, making fluttery noises about the provision of coffee, receiving Francesco's softly spoken rejection of the offer. The faint smile that failed to reach his eyes hid impatience. He must think they were all pathetic!

Taking her time about it, Anna stood, swung her chair around to face the table, impeded by her bulk, and eventually sat.

Across the table her father raised his head just a little. He looked anxious, cowed. Anna couldn't understand it. He was usually so good with people—cheerful and outgoing even when speaking to his creditors, full of his plans, so ebullient. Even the most hard-nosed amongst them had—probably reluctantly, given his track record—believed the energetic William Maybury would get over what he blithely termed a 'temporary blip', and come good.

So what was it about the Italian that made him look as if he was trying to shrink into himself? It should be the other way around, with Dad showing Francesco Mastroianni the door because he knew how he'd treated his daughter.

All those months ago she'd found him pottering about in the greenhouse he'd constructed out of old planks and polythene. 'Dad—while I was on holiday I met this fantastic Italian—Francesco. I'm crazy about him! And it's unbelievable, but he feels the same way about me! He's just phoned. He's in England to see me. He'll arrive this evening. But, listen—I'm catering for a WI meeting in the village hall, so I shan't be here. Until I get back make him comfortable, will you? And don't bore him with all that safari park stuff!'

She hadn't been able to hide the fact that she was almost delirious with happiness, that she was fathoms-deep in love for the first time in her life.

So Dad knew what Francesco done, and yet he couldn't raise a single objection to being bossed around in his own home—much less stick up for his wronged daughter and show the black-hearted devil the door!

So it was up to her! Glancing swiftly at the man who had mangled her heart, who was lording it at the head of the table—where else?—she said flatly, 'Well? If you have something to say, get on with it. Some of us have things to do.'

He ignored her. Leaning forward, long fingers laced on the table-top, he addressed her parents. Anna Maybury, who had once meant all the world to him, now meant nothing except as the carrier of his child. Her wishes in this matter were unimportant, not to be considered.

'Your daughter is carrying my child. We met when she was staying on Ischia.' His mobile mouth hardened as his eyes pinned down William's. 'As of course you know. My point is that as the mother of my child your daughter is now my responsibility.'

'Now, look here!' Incensed by that out-dated assumption, the pointed way he was excluding her from the dialogue, Anna tried to cut him down to size, to point out that she was an adult woman and responsible for herself. But she subsided, red-faced, when he turned his attention to her mother, speaking as if her interjection had no more meaning than the irritating buzz of a fly.

'You must agree, Beatrice—I may call you Beatrice?—that it is not wise for a woman in the latter stages of pregnancy to be working hard all hours of the day, rushing around in hot kitchens until late at night?'

He was turning on that devastating charm now, and her mother was lapping it up, Anna noted sickly. Her eyes bright, her mouth curving with pleasure, no doubt she was enjoying the fact that she now knew the identity of the father of her coming grandchild. 'Don't think I haven't said as much myself, dozens of times!' the older woman concurred quickly. 'She works too hard—and it worries me—but she won't listen. She was always stubborn, even as a baby!'

Thanks a bunch! Anna ground her teeth. So, OK, Mum *had* regularly twittered on about the long hours she worked. But, as Anna had pointed out, they needed the money she earned just to survive. No way was she going to repeat that incontrovertible fact and shame her family, highlight their dire poverty, in front of this brute. He was a stranger to financial problems—would have no idea how it felt to have creditors breathing down his neck.

'So, as I am responsible, Anna will stay at my London home until the birth. I shall not be there, except on the odd occasion, but my excellent housekeeper and her husband will look after her every need,' Francesco stated, with a blithe disregard for any opinion *she* might have. 'She will have every possible care, and the rest she needs for the well-being of the child. Arrangements will be made to have her admitted to a private clinic when the time comes. After the birth—' his eyes swept between her parents '—I will organise a meeting between our respective solicitors to set up a trust to provide for the child's upbringing, schooling and general future welfare.'

'That's very decent of you, old chap.'

Her father was finally showing some signs of life! Anna thought furiously. She scrambled to her feet awkwardly, met the brooding, chilling distance of Francesco's steely eyes and finally got to say her piece.

'Save your breath! I'm going nowhere with you. I

don't want your hand-outs—in fact I never want to see or hear from you again!' And she swept out with as much dignity as her swollen feet and a huge stomach could contrive.

She fumed as she hauled herself up the stairs to her room. How dared he come here and lay the law down? Who did he think he was?

Their brief and to him meaningless holiday fling—which he had already insultingly insinuated the he regretted—had resulted in a new life, but that didn't mean he had any rights. He had forfeited any rights when he'd dumped her!

Indignation kept her going until she reached the chilly sanctuary of her bedroom. Her legs feeling like ill-set jelly, she sank down on the bed and wearily reflected on all she had to do this morning.

Retrieve her van. It would have been accomplished by now if the odious Italian hadn't put his oar in. Pick up provisions in the village. Pay Nick's father for the battery. Phone Kitty Bates to clarify the final number of guests expected at her son's birthday party on Tuesday. Get hold of Cissie and make sure she'd be available to help out. Normally Anna wouldn't turn a hair at catering a kids' party solo, but thanks to the traumatic experience of what had happened over the past dozen or so hours every scrap of energy had left her. And even though Cissie boasted that her culinary expertise went no further than putting bread in the toaster, she was a huge help when it came to fetching and carrying.

Shivering, Anna pulled the quilt over her shoulders and bit back tears of emotional exhaustion. Thinking of

Cissie brought back memories she'd tried and mostly succeeded in wiping from her mind. Memories she didn't want. But…

CHAPTER FOUR

PEACE at last! Anna wriggled her hips further into the warm pebbles and stretched out in the sun. Bliss! All she could hear was the hiss and suck of the clear Italian sea against the shore, and the occasional cry of a seabird.

For the first time since she and Cissie had arrived on Ischia three days ago she felt relaxed and comfortably normal.

To be perfectly honest the hotel they were staying in intimidated her. Silly of her—but it *was* horrendously expensive, with every extravagance laid on for its pampered, seriously wealthy guests. Elegance and sybaritic luxury stretched as far as the eye could see—from the choice of four indoor and outdoor pools, to the coffee shops, formal dining areas, bars, designer boutiques, saunas, right down to the complimentary perfumed essences and soaps in the sumptuous bathroom she and Cissie were sharing.

In her cheap clothes, with her deeply regrettable but entirely understandable air of gobsmacked awe, she stuck out like a sore thumb. She knew she did. It was all right for Cissie, the spoiled and treasured only child of wealthy parents. She dovetailed beautifully with the silk and cashmere set. Cissie, with her sleek, waist-length auburn hair and model figure, her lovely clothes, fitted in. She spoke their language and instinctively knew how to mingle with what the Olds called the jet set. She knew how to have discreet fun on the other side of the tracks!

Only this morning, while covering her micro-bikini with a colourful sarong, Cissie had said, 'Lighten up, Anna. Look—there's no need for you to mope around on your own. I could get Aldo to fix you up, no probs. Just say the word.'

'What word? And who's Aldo?' Anna, glancing up from one of the tasteful complimentary glossies, had wanted to know, and had received an eye-rolling response. 'Aldo—he's serviced our table every evening—even *you* must at least have noticed him!'

A slim Sardinian with coal-black eyes and a dazzling smile. 'You're dating *him*?' Anna made the connection, green eyes widening as her best friend grinned at her.

'Nothing serious—as if! Just a fling—holiday fun! You should try it. It doesn't hurt!' She tossed sunscreen, lipgloss and designer sunglasses into a scarlet cotton beach bag. 'He said he could get you fixed up. Now, I simply must fly. I'm meeting him in the village square— it's strictly against the rules for him to socialise with the guests, apparently. Anyway, think about the offer—you could use some fun.'

'No, thanks.' Anna knew she sounded like a repressive ancient aunt as Cissie left the room, but she wasn't interested in meaningless flings—sex for the sake of it. It made her shudder just to think of it.

Call her old-fashioned, but she equated sex with love. And when she fell in love—and one day she hoped to— it would be for keeps.

Muttering to herself, she got into her plain black one-piece, covered up with a silky shawl Cissie had lent her, and escaped the rarefied atmosphere of the hotel, wishing she had never agreed to come.

'Don't you dare say no!' Cissie had ordered. 'It's a freebie. My parents booked the package—flights, transfers, a fab hotel for three weeks. Only Ma went and broke her leg, didn't she? So they can't go. It's all paid for, and you haven't any bookings on the horizon that you've told me about, so there's nothing to stop you coming along and keeping me company—is there?'

At the time the idea of a free holiday had seemed like a good idea—a chance to escape from what was going on at home. Her dad up to his eyes in debt. Again. There was no more land to sell to keep the creditors at bay. She loved her father to pieces, but wished he was more grounded. His latest 'sure-fire winner' of a scheme was to turn the remaining ten acres of long-neglected gardens into a safari park.

'I just need the right backer,' he'd said when he'd expounded this latest money-spinning plan. 'Can't lose!' When had Anna heard that before? 'Fantastic opportunity for the right investor. We'll get hordes of visitors— rake it in!'

Anna had nightmare visions of mangy old lions eating the giraffes or—heaven forbid—the paying visitors, and tried not to have hysterics.

Of course it wouldn't happen. Dad could charm blood

out of a stone, but not even an out-and-out idiot would put money into such a ridiculous venture.

So they would lose Rylands, Mum's family home, and it would kill her. She had a mental vision of them living in a tiny bungalow, with Dad setting up a chicken farm—or even a pig farm—in a pocket-sized back garden and she shuddered again. Mum would pine for the glory days before she'd married, when her parents had been alive and Rylands had been up there with the very best country houses, complete with indoor and outdoor staff and the comfort of a vast portfolio of stocks and shares. A portfolio Dad had decided to double, but had ended up losing the lot.

Now the hoped-for escape looked like being an uncomfortable experience. Especially as Cissie would be occupied with having fun with her waiter during his off-duty times, leaving Anna to kick her heels around in a hotel where she felt as out of place as a pork pie on a silver dish of caviar.

So she wouldn't stay around—the object of curious stares, the Cinderella in the corner.

Skirting the centre of the village, she stopped to buy fruit and bottled water, and trudged up a rocky incline, wandering through little terraced orchards of fig and lemon trees. She clambered over a low stone wall to a stretch of herb-strewn grassland, alive with butterflies and bees, passing a tiny, lone stone building with its windows open to catch the air, revelling in the uncomplicated, unglitzy rightness of the scents of earth and sea, the warmth of the sun and the endless silent blue arch of the sky.

She came to a narrow track that led down to a secluded cove—a rocky, sheltering headland where deep water lapped with Mediterranean indolence and the pebble beach was devoid of glitterati—of anyone at all.

Perfect.

She wriggled again, relaxed and comfy, on her bed of sun-warmed rounded pebbles, closing her eyes, letting the sun lap her exposed limbs. She could spend all her days here, no problem—eat her fruit lunch, cool off in the sea, catch up with her reading and then join up with Cissie for the evening meal and be entertained—or not—by accounts of the slim Sardinian's sexual expertise, while he served them with smiling obsequiousness.

Drifting between sleep and dreaming, Anna drew her brows together as an alien scraping, rattling noise punctuated by the sound of male voices shattered her solitude. Peering between her tangled lashes she registered the intruders. A shortish, plumpish guy dressed in what were obviously designer casuals stood on the shore, while another dragged a dinghy clear of the water.

The other man was something else, she noted, her eyes widening. Bronzed, at least six foot, clad only in a pair of beat-up old denim cut-offs, he had the type of body—honed, toned, lithe and yet power-packed—that her only experience of was cinematic.

Smiling to herself, she closed her eyes again, waiting for them to go some place else. Voices drifted over on the still, sea-scented air. Italian. She couldn't understand a word of what was being said, of course, but the tone of one of them positively vibrated with authority.

The smartly dressed one thanking the boatman for the trip round the bay, or whatever? The other—the dishy boatman?—was definitely more subservient.

Feet crunched through the pebbles, and curiosity raised her lashes one more time. The smartly dressed one was heading for the zig-zagging path that had brought her down here. Good. The hunk would no doubt be following at a respectful distance.

Silence again. Lovely!

Anna closed her eyes against the glare of the sun and relaxed back into blissful solitude—or tried to. But her skin had started to prickle strangely all over, as if she were plugged into the mains. It couldn't be just the effects of the sun, because there was a weird tingling inside her, too.

'You are on private property.'

Wired as she was, the grating, slightly accented tones made her yelp with shock, sit up, and make a grab for Cissie's silk shawl, her picnic in its tatty plastic bag, her old canvas shoes, her book.

Watching her fumble with the plastic carrier, snatch up the fat paperback and drop it, Francesco regretted the harshness of his tone.

Regret was a stranger to him. His decisions, actions, his tone of voice, tailored to specific situations, were always perfectly judged.

But, standing over her while she'd been supposedly unaware of his presence, he'd taken in the voluptuous contours of a body boldly emphasised by the plain black swimwear, the riotous length of silky sugar-blonde hair, the cute face, the sinfully thick and long lashes, dark but tipped with gold, and had felt his mouth curl with cynicism.

They were everywhere. As he knew from long and tedious experience. They played every trick in the book. They were so predictable. So boring. This particular gold-digger, unable to attract his attention, wangle an introduction, whatever, had decided to drape herself on his private beach. And hope.

And yet...

He'd fully expected her to give him the full works. The sultry look, for starters. That was a given. Then raise her arms above her head, move that sensational body explicitly, lave her lips with the tip of a moist pink tongue and make insincere apologies. Huskily.

Seen it all. Heard it all. He prepared to spell out his uninterest. Brutally, if necessary.

And yet she had squawked like a cat with its tail caught in a door. Scrambled for her scattered belongings without grace or dignity. Or pretence at either. And now she was standing, a good head shorter than he was, clutching a bunch of material in front of her. Hiding, not displaying, with a plastic carrier dangling from the hand that wasn't struggling to arrange the fabric for the best possible concealment.

Maybe, just maybe, he'd made a mistake. There was a first time for everything.

Sable brows drew together as she raised her eyes to his. Green and deep enough to drown in. Part-fascinated, and part-ashamed of his cynical assumptions, he watched as hot colour touched her skin in a wave of mortification as she managed chokily, 'I'm sorry. I had no idea this was private property. I'll go.'

Anna had never felt so disorientated in the whole of

her life. That harsh voice, the condemnatory words, had exploded onto her consciousness when she had believed herself alone. It had really spooked her. So much so that an automatic reflex action had had her practically leaping to her feet and floundering around for her scattered belongs, adrenaline pumping.

And now, actually looking at the guy, she felt a slow, hot fizzle start up inside her. Instinctive—because he really was something else. Too much. Too male, too bronzed, too knock-'em-dead-handsome, with that tousled silky black hair, penetrating smoke-grey eyes, aristocratic nose, razor-sharp cheekbones and a mouth so sensual it made her knees go weak and her breath bunch in her throat.

And as for that physique…

Anna swallowed thickly and dipped her head, ashamed of the heated colour that was burning her face. She turned to go, stumbled, was stayed by a strong, long-fingered hand on her arm. She trembled with the wicked intensity of the sensations that skittered through her entire body at the sizzling contact

'There's no need to go.'

'But you said—' Her voice sounded like a frog with a sore throat. She clamped her mouth shut and shivered again, despite the heat of the sun.

'I know what I said.'

He sounded gently amused now—an improvement on that authoritative bite. Anna flicked a sideways glance, her eyes colliding with the broad expanse of his perfectly honed, bronzed torso, with the 'gold' chain round his neck that left telltale green marks where it touched his so-touchable satin-smooth skin.

No rich playboy, then! No playboy worth the name would be seen dead wearing something that cheap and nasty! Just ordinary—like her! If such a charismatic specimen could ever be classed as ordinary! Emboldened, she raised her eyes, met his. Warm, smoky grey with dancing silver lights. Smiling eyes now.

'But I happen to know the owner is on holiday, and I'm sure he wouldn't want your day to be spoiled.'

Francesco released her arm. He'd made a mistake. Now he had to make amends. In his comprehensive experience of gold-diggers they never blushed. Wouldn't know how. Bold-faced to a woman. As his mother had been. Not content with bleeding his blinkered father dry, she'd broken his heart when she'd taken off with a far better financial prospect after the reality that the cash was drying up had hit.

Not willing to go there, he turned his attention back to the unwitting trespasser, still pink-cheeked and clearly uncomfortable. His sensual mouth quirked. 'I take it you prefer solitude to crowded beaches?'

Anna expelled a long breath and found herself smiling and nodding. Rather inanely, she was afraid.

True, this guy had given her a real fright to begin with—had made her want to scurry for cover before the heavy mob moved in to escort her from someone's private property. But now he seemed nice and ordinary—no, she amended, extraordinary. And despite that initial chilling note of authority he was actually being really gentle as he removed the shawl from her slackened fingers, then the carrier, dropped them to one side and invited, 'Please make yourself comfortable again. Enjoy the day.'

She had a spectacular body. Lush curves, a too-enticing cleavage, a waist he could span with both hands with room to spare. His brow furrowed. 'Look, don't take this personally, but there are some pretty dodgy characters around. A lone attractive woman could be at risk.'

'Attractive' didn't cut it. She was lovely—hair, face and body to die for. Annoyingly, he felt something kick hard in his loins. *Basta!* That was not what he wanted. The women he bedded, when he could be bothered to take up the invitation, knew the score. He had never touched a wide-eyed innocent, and everything about the trespasser told him she was exactly that. Which was why he had suddenly become protective, he rationalised. The thought of one of the young men on the prowl latching on to her, all sweet words and empty promises, seducing her, made him metaphorically clench his fists.

But she'd be safe here. The local Lotharios knew better than to trespass on his property, and visitors tended, sheep-like, to herd together on the public beaches, and in the cafés and shopping areas.

Anna was tempted to take him at his word. She craved solitude, the opportunity to laze around and relax, to clear her head of worries about what was happening back home. It was the only way she could hope to return to England refreshed and able to face the problems, somehow cope with them.

'You're sure the owner—whoever—wouldn't mind?' she pressed. 'You're not just saying that?' She didn't want bother. Bother didn't gel with the bliss of a long unwinding session on a sun-soaked deserted beach.

A slow smile curved his sensual mouth. 'You have my word. I know the owner very well.'

The boat, beached on the shore, seemed to bear this out. He obviously must have permission to use the cove. 'Right. Thanks.' Anna's smile was sunny as she arranged herself back in the comfy nest she'd made in the pebbles, then faded as she saw he was on the point of leaving.

She didn't want him to go. Not giving herself time to analyse how strange that was, she dipped her hand into the carrier and held out a couple of plump peaches. 'Have one? Rowing a boat must be thirsty work.'

There'd been no sound of an engine. Maybe he couldn't afford an outboard? It was the *faux* gold chain that did it, she decided, as her heart flipped. It made her feel all mushy inside. Sort of achingly protective—like a mother who saw a kid of hers trying to keep up with the big boys and failing because he had no street cred. He was unaware that the flashy gold chain left green stains on his skin which shouted out *Brass!* It was crazy, because in every other respect this hunk had everything. Plus.

'*Grazie.*' Mildly surprised at himself, Francesco took a peach and found himself wondering if her skin felt the same—soft, firm, warmly seductive. Just humouring her, he excused himself, and sank down beside her. 'You are English? You are staying here on the island?' he asked.

Nodding her affirmative, peach juice dribbling down her chin, Anna named the hotel and saw his spectacular eyes narrow. She felt immediately uncomfortable.

Being a local, he would know that it cost an arm and a leg just to walk through the doors.

She was about to launch into an explanation of how

she came to be staying there when he said, in a rough-ened undertone, '*Madre di Dio!* You remind me!' He was on his feet, smiling down at her. 'My—some people are waiting there for me to give them a tour of the island. *Scusi*—' He was walking away, sunlight glistening on those wide bronzed shoulders. 'Enjoy your days here, *signorina.*'

She dreamt of him that night. Which was ridiculous. And woke feeling wired which was quite unlike her normally pragmatic self.

Should she go to the private cove again? Or not?

Would he put in an appearance?

Her tummy flipped alarmingly.

He'd need to collect his boat if he'd found punters wanting a trip out to sea. On the other hand he might again be booked as tour guide and not need to go anywhere near the cove.

Over dinner last night, while Cissie had been regaling her with how she and Aldo had spent the day—going some place on the back of his motor scooter—she hadn't been listening properly at all really. Too busy looking at the other diners and wondering which group had hired the gorgeous Italian to show them round the island.

How stupid was that?

She didn't even know his name.

If they passed in the street he wouldn't recognise her, so she had to stop thinking like a teenager in the throes of a silly crush!

She prodded Cissie awake when Room Service arrived with their breakfast. 'Get up!'

Bleary eyes peered through a tangle of rich auburn hair. 'Why the hurry? Where's the fire?'

No hurry. The whole day and what to do with it stretched out before her. And the fire was here, right inside her, a sort of fiery fever.

'It's another lovely day,' she said inanely, crossing to the side table and pouring coffee into two wide bowls. Passing one to Cissie, forcing her to sit up to take it, ignoring her grumbles, she asked, half hoping the answer would be negative, 'Are you seeing Aldo today?'

If she wasn't then the poser of whether to take off to the cove again would be answered—the decision taken out of her hands. She and Cissie would spend the day sightseeing, lounging by one of the pools—doing nothing in particular except keeping each other company.

'You bet—weren't you listening? I told you over dinner last night, didn't I? His aunt runs a *pensione*— he lives with her during the season—and he's got this room. Said he'd make lunch for me.' The prospect of the day ahead brightened Cissie's eyes as she dumped her coffee bowl on the night-table and swung her endless legs out of bed, heading for the shower.

Shaking her head, a wry smile on her soft mouth, Anna drank her coffee. Cissie's morals were bang up-to-date, twenty-first-century stuff. While she—well, she was so old-fashioned she was in danger of turning into a laughing stock.

So what was she doing, scrambling down to the private cove, her heart banging as if it wanted to jump out of her body, her eyes straining to see if the little row-boat was still beached on the shore?

It was.

Slowing her descent, even more jittery inside, she felt her legs like wobbly jelly. Weak-kneed at the sight of a very ordinary boat!

How sad was that?

Well, the guy was fascinating. No question about that. And people were always fascinated by the exotic, weren't they? And she was no different. It wasn't as if she was wanting to have sex with him. Perish the thought! Her face burned at the very idea. She wasn't Cissie. She was practical, sensible, and very, very moral!

To prove it, she thrust him out of her mind and, not in the mood to lounge around in the sun—because she just knew she'd start thinking about him again—headed over the beach to cool off in the sea…

Sorted. Methodically, efficiently sorted. Without giving himself time to think of anything beyond the practical. Alerting his housekeeper to the imminent arrival of a long-stay house guest. Paying a patiently waiting Nick Whoever for the battery, his time and his trouble. Stopping the objection he saw coming from the younger man with a single downward slash of his hand. Arranging for the return of the van to Rylands. Making his excuses to his cousin, ditto the sex-on-legs offering. And leaving.

The future mother of his child would be waiting. A concise phone call to her mother—Beatrice, nice lady—had elicited her agreement that, yes, Anna would be packed and waiting.

There'd been an unspoken yet firm 'or else' about that

agreement. Despite her wispy appearance there was steel in that backbone. He approved of that. And as for the father—well, he'd seemed happy enough with the financial arrangement. He'd been uncomfortable throughout the entire interview, which pointed to the undeniable fact that Anna had put him up to that attempt to squeeze a sizeable amount of money from her besotted lover. Had she promised that it would be a dead cert?

And as for Sweet Anna—definitely cranky. Spluttering about not wanting anything from him. A plain case of saying one thing and meaning another. Grouchy because perhaps she'd expected, eventually, a bigger pay-off?

Or marriage? His eyes narrowed to dark slits as his jaw clenched. A snowflake in hell just about summed up the chances of that!

Navel-gazing, pulling out buried emotions and putting them under a microscope wasn't his style. What was done was done. Lesson learned. Move on.

Yet as he eased the Ferrari out onto the lane the hypnotic rhythm of the windscreen wipers as they cleared the intermittent rain took him back to where he didn't want to be.

That morning.

He'd seen her walk past his holiday hideaway. The Hovel, his sister called it. The private place he went to when he wanted to unwind, to forget he was one of the wealthiest men in Italy with all the pressures, responsibilities and constant calls on his time that went with that status. The place where interruptions were forbidden.

A rule that had been broken for the first time the day before, when his senior aide had arrived nervously bleating about a problem with the Christou takeover, needing his decision. A decision had been made while rowing out to drop lobster pots on the other side of the headland—a trip not relished by his green-gilled employee. Returning to the cove, he'd found his dishy little trespasser, dismissed the older man and then headed off to tell her to take her scheming little self off his property. A mistake. And he'd ended up assuring her she would be welcome any time, hoping he hadn't scared her off for good.

Obviously he hadn't. That had made him feel good. He wasn't used to making mistakes.

That morning she'd worn her glorious hair piled precariously on top of her white-gold head. Tendrils already escaping. The silky fabric thing had been tied around her waist, fluttering unevenly around her shapely calves, and underneath she'd worn the same black swimsuit as before, which caressed her magnificent breasts like a lover's touch.

Did she realise how gorgeous she was? He had wondered. From their brief encounter yesterday he didn't think so. He would put money on her being that rare creature, a woman in—what?—her early twenties, at a guess, who was innocent, unaware.

After ten minutes he had followed her, telling himself he was merely going to assure her, yet again, that it was OK for her to use the cove. Neglecting, of course to tell her he owned it—owned most of the land on this magical corner of the island, plus the hotel where she was staying.

She had been swimming. A sedate breaststroke.

Without questioning the wisdom of what he was doing he had joined her, his racing crawl powerful, and he had enjoyed the flash of surprise in those wide sea-green eyes before a dazzling smile of recognition had lit her water-spangled lovely face.

From then on, without knowing it, he'd been hooked. By her warmth, her beauty, the artlessness that had made his heart melt. Such a thing had never happened to him before, so he'd had no idea what was happening. Had only known that he didn't want the morning to end. Lazy conversation beneath the lazy sun. Abstract, nothing personal apart from the exchange of names. He had watched, narrow-eyed, for the glitter of recognition as he told her his name—a name regularly turning up in frivolous gossip columns or, more soberly, in the international financial pages in London, where he was based for months at a time.

Nothing. She'd had no idea who he was! He had felt like a six-year-old on Christmas morning. And the feeling had been great!

'Yesterday you gave me fruit. Today I will give you pasta. I will cook for you.' Surprised by that invitation, he waited for her reaction. His hideaway was inviolate, private to him, but her company delighted him and he wasn't about to lose it. How serious was that?

The eyes that had been smiling for him were veiled by the intriguing sweep of her lashes. Finally her glorious hair was down, pale silky tendrils parting over her sun-kissed shoulders, a stray corkscrew lying against a cleavage that was more tempting than she could know.

'I have no ulterior motive,' he vowed softly, guessing

she needed that reassurance. Female English tourists were easy game, or so he'd heard. She wasn't like that. 'Merely I enjoy your company.' That was true, wasn't it?

He wasn't sure at all when he reached out his hand to tip her chin, to let his eyes meet hers and impress upon her his trustworthy intentions. The small chin beneath his fingers, the delicacy of bone beneath the soft skin, the visceral shock of registering that this was the first time he'd touched her, the brilliance of the eyes that met his in unquestioning trust, the way those luscious lips parted as she said, 'I'd like that,' almost proved his undoing.

From then on the outcome was inevitable. Starting with the delight she took in his tiny stone cottage. 'This is just perfect! Do you live here all the time?'

'Not all the time,' he prevaricated, feeling like a cad when she nodded solemnly.

'No, I guess work's hard to find out of season. No call for a tour guide if there are no tourists. You'd have to go to the mainland to find work. But, hey! It must be wonderful to know you've got this place to come back to in the spring.'

Her smile dazzled him. So much so he almost came clean there and then. Selfishly, he supposed, he did no such thing. It was fantastic to find a woman who enjoyed his company, liked him for the man he was rather than his bank balance.

More than liked him? A beat of anticipation slammed through his body at the way that soft veil of colour stole into her cheeks whenever their eyes met. Her breath quickened, and the rise and fall of those magnificent breasts beneath the straining black fabric—

His gruff apologies for their scratch meal, a simple salad and pasta, had brought forth, 'It's delicious! The herby sauce is to die for! And I cook for a living— private dinner parties and stuff—so I should know! Of course bookings slow to a standstill during the summer holiday period, which is why I was able to take a break.'

Cue to delve more deeply into her life, her background. He let it go. The only important thing was that somehow, almost without him knowing it, she had become the most entrancing female on the planet.

Inevitable.

Quite how it happened that first time he would never know. One minute she was on the point of leaving— thanking him, smiling for him, gathering the bits and pieces she seemed unable to go anywhere without—the next his hands were touching her. Her warm silky shoulders. And her hands touched him. Splayed out against his chest, where his heart was beating a furious tattoo.

And then frenzy. A white heat explosion inside his head as he kissed her. Her soft mouth opening for him as their bodies meshed. Her fractured moan of surrender as her hips tilted to meet his urgent arousal. And he knew he was entering paradise as somehow they took the stairs, slowly, one by one, entwined, breath straining, reaching the sanctuary of his bed where he found true heaven, found love, for the first time in his life.

That she had been a virgin, that no thought of using protection had entered his head, he'd accepted without a single qualm. He had found the woman he wanted to spend the rest of his life with.

CHAPTER FIVE

IT WAS well into the afternoon—dull and rainy now, which suited her mood perfectly—when Anna heard the growl of Francesco's arrival. No doubt about it. Trust him to drive that in-your-face piece of costly ego-massaging machinery!

Her stomach feeling like a lead balloon, she picked up her bag of toiletries and followed her father as he carried her suitcase downstairs. She'd been left alone until lunchtime—alone with all that counter-productive backwards-peering stuff—when Mum had walked into her bedroom.

'Time to stop sulking. Lunch first, then you must pack. Francesco will pick you up at around four.'

So when had Mum decided to put on the first brisk act of her life? It would have been a subject of amazement—like watching a house mouse turn round and punch the cat on its nose—if it hadn't been so annoying.

'If you imagine I'm going anywhere with him, you've got rocks in your head!'

'Now, don't be childish! It's not like you, Anna. I know this morning's been a shock—for all of us—but you must have thought he was special once. He is the father of your baby, after all.'

Not something she wanted remotely to be reminded of!

'Your father and I had a long chat with him after you walked out in a huff. He's taking his responsibilities seriously, Anna. He's determined that you have a complete rest before the birth—he does have a vested interest in the well-being of his child, after all—and in that I agree with him entirely. I've been telling you for weeks that running yourself ragged can't be good for you or your baby. In my opinion, and your father's, he's a man of integrity.'

He wouldn't know integrity from a hole in the street!

'He assured us that you would have the best care possible, and that a top-flight obstetrician would be privately engaged at his expense—all the things it would be impossible for us to provide. And to set our minds at rest he'll send a car and driver to pick your father and me up tomorrow, so that we can stay with you for a couple of days and satisfy ourselves that all is as it should be. And while we're there with you he'll have his lawyer draw up some document or other, stating the amount that will be paid into your account each month to provide for the maintenance of the child, which is right and proper. So many unmarried fathers shirk their responsibility.'

Give the devil his due, he knew how to press all the right buttons! He had obviously got her parents right on side. There was no earthly use explaining how he had made a fool of her and then betrayed her. It would only make her folks even more determined to see that he paid for his bad behaviour.

But was she to have no input at all? It was her baby, her body. She was not about to be packed up like a parcel, picked up and plonked down some place she didn't want to be. So—

'Very neat. Very businesslike. But, tell me, how are you and Dad going to manage without my financial contributions?' Not huge, not even middleweight, but they kept the wolf from the door. It wasn't something she had ever rubbed their noses in, but desperate times called for desperate measures.

'That's all taken care of. He's given your father a cheque to cover your loss of income for the next six months. A very generous one, too, if I may say so.'

After more of the same Anna had simply thrown in the towel. Truth was, she had been feeling exhausted for weeks, putting a brave face on her situation and trying not to worry about her baby's well-being. And the unprecedented spat with her mother had left her feeling like yesterday's used teabag.

Taking it easy for the next few weeks could only benefit her unborn child, and she had to admit that she would do almost anything to feel less exhausted and anxious about the prospect of single parenthood. It would be achievable, just about—if Francesco lived up to what he'd said about not being around much himself.

Even so, she wasn't going to give him the satisfaction of letting him know how completely she'd caved in. So she straightened her drooping spine and gave him her coldest glare when she came face to face with him in the vast, echoing hall.

He looked as spectacular as ever, drat him! A

superbly tailored dark grey silk and mohair suit draped those wide shoulders, long legs and narrow hips. It was a perfectly groomed specimen—from his expertly styled dark hair to the pristine white shirt that emphasised the rich olive tones of his skin and the shadowing on his tough jawline. The cool silver eyes were partly veiled by long thick lashes as he registered her appearance, and her steps faltered at the totally unwanted reminder that she knew, intimately, every magnificent inch of that unfairly superb body.

A sting of sexual excitement surged through her, unwelcome and out-of-place, and had her walking out of the open main door, oblivious to the burblings and twitterings of her respective parents. She let herself into his car, with some difficulty because of her bulk, and waited.

The moment he joined her, not even bothering to look at her, much less speak, she levelled at him, 'I'm doing this under protest. As long as you understand that.'

'Really?' He fired the ignition. His classically handsome profile was as arid as his tone had been. 'Protesting about what? The financial arrangements? Your parents seemed satisfied.'

'Well, they would be.' Anna slumped back into her seat as the sleek machine nosed out onto the narrow lane. He would be paying maintenance for his child, and that, in their eyes, would be right and proper. Quite enough. But for her... 'It's not enough.' Unconsciously she voiced her thoughts aloud, uselessly wishing her unborn child could have a proper father—one who loved them both, was there for them on a permanent basis, one who didn't think that money was the only thing that counted.

'I rather thought not.' His tone was dry as dust. 'But there's no more on offer. I made a mistake, and I accept the responsibility that goes with it. I will support the child financially and that's my final offer.'

Too full of loathing to speak, Anna screwed her hands into fists and stared unseeingly through the windscreen, hating him so much she felt physically sick. Vilely, he'd taken it as read that she'd meant she wanted more of his wretched money!

And 'a mistake'! How demeaning was that? He was cynically referring to that first time. When he'd been too overcome by lust to give a thought to contraception, and she'd been too overwhelmed by the awesome sensation of falling in love for the first time in her life to even think of repercussions.

That had been the mistake he now regretted. Hadn't repeated. Oh, no! He'd reined in that animal lust sufficiently to use protection after that.

And his protestations of love had only been made to make sure that he was able to come back for more of the same while she was on the island. Fervent protestations that had fooled her into believing that she had gone to heaven.

Lying louse!

And to think that she had actually been formulating plans to join him in Italy—maybe start a small restaurant together, live hand-to-mouth if necessary. How foolish had that been? That had been before she'd discovered what he'd so carefully hidden—that he was mega-rich. Concealing it from her because he was afraid that she might try to get her hands on some of his wealth!

So let him go on thinking she was miffed because the future maintenance for their child wasn't nearly enough for her. No way would she make an even bigger fool of herself in his eyes and confess that when that unguarded comment had slipped out she'd been wistfully thinking of a proper family—mother, father and child, all loving and caring for each other, all that soppy happy-ever-after stuff! He would laugh until his head fell off!

Men like him—liars and cheats—automatically thought the worst of everyone else. It was beyond a simple, straightforward soul like her to try to change that entrenched view of humankind. So she wouldn't waste her breath trying.

'You need to change your attitude,' he spelt out in a voice as cold as ice. 'You gave it your best shot, but you failed. Accept it and stop acting like a spoiled child who's found out it can't have everything it wants. While you're staying at my London home you will treat my housekeeper Peggy Powell and her husband Arnold with the respect they deserve. I expect to see no more rude and objectionable behaviour.' He gave her a withering glance. 'You can be sweet and charming when you want to be—as I know to my cost.'

Francesco's brow clenched ferociously as he belatedly registered that slip of the tongue. Where had that come from? As far as he was concerned the past was dead—another country he could walk away from and forget—so why refer to it? Yet another mistake, he recognised savagely. Around her he was making too many of them, he castigated.

Then a small explosion came from his side, as she

picked up and repeated, '*To your cost?* That's rich! I doubt you'll even notice the money you pay out for our baby!'

'Our baby.' When had she started bracketing them together as parents? Anna thought. When she'd believed his lies about loving her more than his life she would have joyously accepted that bond, believing they had a future together. Knowing how foolishly gullible she'd been and how much he'd hurt her lowered her even more than his earlier holier-than-thou diatribe had infuriated her.

Receiving that explosive little speech, Francesco let his lean hands relax on the steering wheel. So he hadn't betrayed the hurt she'd dished out, as he'd feared. She'd discounted the emotional cost. It probably hadn't entered her mind. She had homed in on the financial aspect—as she and others of her kind always would.

The relief Anna felt when they finally reached their destination, after a silent journey punctuated only by those early acrimonious exchanges, was tempered by a serious butterfly attack.

She might have known that his home would be an elegant Regency townhouse in a quiet London square, positively oozing discreet wealth and power, but it wasn't that which was making her feel so jittery.

Would the Powells, into whose care she was apparently to be given, treat her like a stray cat their employer had misguidedly picked up from the gutter? Or like a fallen woman, ditto?

In either event she wouldn't be able to stand it, and would be on the first train back home!

'Come.' Impatience spiked the command as Francesco swept past her, carrying her suitcase, and Anna, her soft mouth mutinous, followed. So she was an encumbrance he couldn't wait to rid himself of? So what else was new? It didn't hurt—how could it, when she wanted to see the back of him too?—so why did she suddenly want to cry her eyes out?

The weird hormonal chaos of pregnancy, she sensibly assured herself, blinking the moisture from her eyes as she watched the imposing glossy black-painted door swing open. It revealed a tiny woman wearing a starchy black dress, her iron-grey hair cut as short as a boy's, but the wideness of her greeting smile negated the severities of her appearance.

'Peggy, I'm sorry I'm late. A few hold-ups, I'm afraid.'

His voice was warm, as it once had been for her, and his arm lay easily across his housekeeper's spare shoulders. Anna felt the chill of exclusion shiver through her bones.

He turned, 'Peggy, meet Anna Maybury. As I told you, she is in need of rest and relaxation, and I look to you to provide it.'

She felt quite horribly embarrassed, expecting a sniffy flicker of those button eyes in her direction, and almost sagged with relief when she found herself on the receiving end of a generously warm smile. 'I shall enjoy that! Come in, Anna, do. I've kept dinner back, but I expect you'll want to freshen up first. I'll show you to your room, my dear. Arnold!'

As if her voice had brought him into being, a man as large as his wife was small silently appeared, smiling a greeting for Anna, taking her suitcase from his employer and heading for the imposing staircase.

'Anna will eat in her room when she's settled,' Francesco said. 'I'll just take a sandwich and coffee in my study. I'm leaving for the States first thing in the morning, and I have a raft of work to get through before then. And, Peggy, don't bother packing for me. I'll see to it.'

Not a word for her. Not one, Anna noted as he walked away. She didn't know whether to feel belittled, hurt, or just plain relieved. But what had she expected? A fond farewell? A promise to look in on her later to make sure she was comfortable in strange surroundings, had everything she wanted?

Oh, get real! she grumped at herself as she accepted Peggy's invitation to follow her. This was a man who mightily disliked the situation he found himself in, but who, to prevent any future claims on his wealth, was making sure he could never be accused of shirking his responsibilities regarding the well-being of mother and child. He'd be having some hotshot lawyer draw up a watertight document spelling out exactly what she and the child would be entitled to and what they were not.

Fact.

So him ignoring her existence—leaving for the States and probably not coming near his London home again until he heard from the Powells that his son or daughter had arrived and that mother and child were back at Rylands—was a relief, she assured herself as, feeling impossibly drained, she followed where Peggy led. Being around him was too emotionally traumatic. So his absence would be considerably more beneficial than his presence.

* * *

A week to go—give or take! A quiver of excitement started in the region of her heart and shot down to her toes. Soon she would hold her baby in her arms.

The garden at the rear of the house was a surprising green and floriferous oasis of tranquillity in the heart of the restless city. Arnold looked after it beautifully, and Anna liked to help where she could—dead-heading, mostly, it being the only task the older man thought suitable for a heavily pregnant lady!

She liked to breakfast on the terrace when the weather was fine, and this morning it was spectacularly beautiful.

'Did you sleep well?' Peggy asked as she transferred tea things, orange juice and toast from the tray she carried to the teak table.

'On and off.' Anna smiled. This late in her pregnancy it was almost impossible to get comfortable in bed.

'Not long now.' The tray emptied, the housekeeper held it against her board-flat bosom. 'Sir Willoughby-Burne is very pleased with you, and you'll remember what he said, won't you?'

'That I must tell you the moment the contractions start and Arnold will drive me to the clinic,' she trotted out robotically. Then, catching Peggy's slight frown, she smiled. 'Sorry—of course I'll remember!' She had endured endless tests and proddings at the elegantly urbane obstetrician's instigation—Sir Willoughby-Burne didn't believe in half measures—and had been given a guided tour round a clinic that had left her speechless, because it seemed more like a five-star hotel than a maternity hospital. Which all went to verify the fact that Francesco was sparing no expense in the execution of his duties—as he saw them.

Tears momentarily blinded her as Peggy took her leave. Her baby's father should be the one she went to when the baby decided to make an appearance. He should be the one to drive her to hospital! To stay with her!

Despising herself for that piece of downright mawkishness, she reached for the glass of orange juice. Her teeth chattered against the rim. She put it down again. What was the matter with her? Of course Peggy and Arnold would be the ones she would turn to. Ever since she'd arrived here they'd looked after her, treated her like a cross between a cherished daughter and a valued house guest. While The Louse hadn't shown his face—hadn't even made contact with her. He had only phoned occasionally, apparently, for a progress report from his housekeeper—largely, Anna suspected, to check that she wasn't being 'rude and objectionable'!

Her hand shaking, she poured tea into the pretty china cup.

'Aren't you going to eat your toast?' he said.

The teapot hit the table-top with a clatter. Her breath left her. Lungs starved of oxygen, she twisted round. How long had he been standing there, at the open French windows, watching her? And why did he look so lethally attractive?

A treacherous leap of sexual excitement assaulted her, destroying what was left of her self-esteem. How could her body react that way to the man who had so callously set out to seduce her, make her fall so deeply in love with him she had been in danger of drowning, and then cold-bloodedly dump her?

Riven by emotions she couldn't begin to name, she watched him walk to where she was sitting, her heartbeats going crazy. That glossy dark head, so proudly held, the smoky and unreadable eyes. The impeccable suiting enhancing those broad shoulders, narrow hips and long powerful legs. So effortlessly elegant, so impossibly remote.

But he hadn't always been remote. Angrily, she shook her head. She wouldn't let herself be reminded of the way it had once been, because it had been a lie as far as he was concerned.

A tanned, strongly lean hand pulled out a chair. He sat. 'You don't want me to join you. You shake your head at me.'

'I can't stop you.' She didn't meet his eyes. She couldn't. Her only defence against this awful awareness of his shocking sexuality and the effect it was having on her had to be a façade of dull indifference.

'True.'

He had the gall to sound amused! Anna swiped the top off her egg as if she were biting his head off his shoulders, and almost choked on the first mouthful as he drawled, 'I see your temper hasn't improved. But your appearance has. You look much better—less exhausted. And beautiful, of course.'

'Yeah. Right.' Sarky monster! 'Beautiful' applied to leggy model-types. She could understand that. To wallowing lumps—no way! Giving up all pretence at eating, she glared at him. 'Why are you here?'

'It is my home. Or one of them. And I wanted to know if you'd signed that agreement—if your parents were satisfied that the child's future security was adequately provided for.'

'Perfectly adequately,' she responded, unable to stop a reminiscent grin flickering across her piquant features. And if he thought she looked like the cat that had got at the cream, tough. He would find out soon enough that she'd taken one look at the monthly payment proposed and had had that hotshot lawyer reduce the amount by three-quarters before she agreed to sign. She wanted the security of knowing that if her business failed or even faltered her child's basic needs would be provided for. She didn't want to live in the lap of luxury at his expense!

'Good.' His tone was hard, and he made a visible effort to rein back the cynical comment that he was glad to learn that she'd finally decided to cut her losses and settle for what she could get out of him. Out of deference to her condition he said, 'And did your parents enjoy their brief stay here?'

Anna nodded. She wasn't going to go into that. The way her mother had positively drooled over his beautiful home, over the valuable paintings and lovely antiques—doubtless recalling the things that had once graced Rylands and had had to be sold to repay debts or finance some hare-brained scheme of her father's. Or the way she'd said, 'It's sad, but we have to face it. We can't expect Francesco to do the decent thing and marry you. A man in his position will have the pick of all the independently wealthy society beauties around.'

As Francesco gazed at her profile, at the suddenly vulnerable droop of her mouth, her original question came back to badger him. If he was truthful, he didn't know why he was here. His firm intention had been to steer clear until he received news from Peggy that she had been delivered of the child and that, after a suitable interval, was being driven back to Rylands and the care of her parents. At which point, knowing that he had fulfilled his responsibilities in respect of financial support, he would forget he'd ever met her.

But something unknown had driven him to alter his plans. To be with her for the birth? To support and comfort her? No way! His body tensed in utter repudiation of that idiotic notion.

To satisfy himself that everything was going well because the child she was carrying was his and he needed to know—despite the reassuring updates he'd had from his housekeeper—that she had lost that frightening look of bone-deep tiredness? Quite possibly. More than likely, in fact. Certainly much nearer the truth than that other insane thought. Because he wasn't heartless. Or not completely.

Satisfied with that explanation for his unannounced visit, he relaxed, veiled his eyes. Watched her.

It was true, despite her patent disbelief. She was beautiful. All that glorious silky pale hair framing her lovely face, that peachy skin glowing with health now, the huge sparkling deep green eyes and gold-tipped lashes—even her swollen body had a beauty that touched him deeply. His eyes welded to the sinful curve of that luscious pink mouth—the only feature that belied the impression of angelic innocence, an innocence designed to capture the unwary.

Desire surged through him and he briefly closed his eyes, his teeth clenching. *Dio mio!* He was no longer unwary! He knew what she was—a scheming, avaricious witch, clever enough to use an act of unworldly innocence to get to him. Unlike the other women who threw themselves at him, dollar signs in neon lights deep in their money-grubbing eyes, recognisable at a hundred paces.

When he looked at her again his eyes were cold. 'Finish your breakfast.' Abruptly pushing back his chair, he walked away.

The birth couldn't come soon enough. One of his security men would be delegated to keep a watching brief on the welfare of the child and report back to him. But he need never to have anything to do with the mother again.

The contractions were ten minutes apart. Anna, sitting on the edge of her bed, pleated her brow. Could a first baby come a week early? And how could you tell if they were false labour pains?

Everything she'd been told at the antenatal clinic flew out of her head. She pushed her feet into her slippers, reached her shabby old mac from the massive wardrobe and grabbed the small case that had been packed for days. Dithering about whether or not she should wake Peggy and Arnold was senseless. They wouldn't hold it against her if it was a false alarm.

But out in the dimly lit corridor a contraction so strong it sent her staggering with shock into a delicate table, sending the china bowl of pot-pourri flying, had her deciding that this was happening. This was real.

Almost immediately two doors opened. Francesco was already pulling on a pair of dark trousers, hopping on one leg, his soft black hair a rumpled tangle, and Peggy was pushing her arms into a quilted housecoat.

'I'll take her, Peggy. Go back to bed.' One look at Anna, an awful old coat over a voluminous cotton night-dress, her smooth brow glistening with beads of sweat, told him all he needed to know. To his housekeeper's protest he said, 'It will save time,' and to Anna, 'Stay there. I'll fetch the car.'

Beyond caring who escorted her, Anna watched him fly down the stairs, pulling a dark blue cashmere sweater over his head as he went, and slowly followed, Peggy's hand on her elbow. The anxious father-to-be. A nice thought, but thoroughly erroneous. He just didn't fancy the idea of her giving birth on the priceless hall carpet.

'He's so perfect!' Anna raised love-drenched eyes from her beautiful baby to his father, past wrongs forgotten in this moment of pure joy.

To her eternal surprise and gratitude Francesco hadn't left her side for one moment, encouraging her, praising her, bossing the medical team as if he knew what she needed and they didn't, holding her hand and mopping her brow. So he had earned this moment of blissful truce.

Awestruck, Francesco touched his newborn son's velvety cheek, saw the big, slightly unfocussed eyes open and meet his, and fell irretrievably in love.

His son. Flesh of his flesh. A lump rose painfully in his throat. How could he ever, for one single moment, have believed he could remain at a distance, never see this tiny miracle's first smile, hear his first word, watch him take his first steps, guide him through his childhood and adolescence, see him safely to manhood?

Madre di Dio! He must have been out of his mind if he'd ever imagined he could give his child up.

He wasn't like his father. He would die before he closed his heart to his son just because his son's mother was a deceitful, avaricious witch!

'I will go and phone the good news through to your parents,' he excused himself gruffly, leaving his precious new son with a wrench, his mind already formulating hard and fast rules for the future.

CHAPTER SIX

THREE weeks later Anna replaced the receiver on its wall mount in the showcase kitchen. She'd been helping Peggy prepare lunch when the call had come through.

'Not bad news?' Peggy looked up from the chopping board, her head tipped to one side.

'Not good.' Dismay made her voice thin. 'My mother—it seems our family home is to be sold.'

Mum had sounded so flat as she'd broken the news. 'I've finally got your father to agree that selling up here is the only way to pay off all those debts. He dug his heels in, of course—it's taken me weeks to persuade him, and I hated having to argue with him, but it had to be done. There'll be nothing left over—what the bank doesn't take, the other creditors will. He'll have to keep that labouring job on, unfortunately, and I'll try to find something, too. We'll have to rent a couple of rooms somewhere. They call it downsizing, don't they?'

Her attempt at breezy humour had brought tears to Anna's eyes, but she'd blinked them away as she listened.

'If you hadn't been so awkward over Francesco's monthly allowance you could easily have afforded to rent a nice cottage for you and little Sholto. You'll have to explain your new circumstances and ask for the full amount to be reinstated.'

Anna hadn't argued with that unwelcome, untenable advice. But asking Francesco anything was a distinct impossibility. She hadn't seen or heard from him since the day after their baby's birth when he'd walked in and told her, while sweeping his sleepy son out of his crib and cuddling him close to his broad accommodating chest, that they had to choose a name together. Now.

She'd accepted his odd command, and they'd finally settled on Sholto, just like proper parents. Since then she'd seen or heard nothing. He'd done what he'd always meant to do—left them behind, walked away. She'd told herself over and over that she'd expected it, so why did she feel as if she'd lost something? It didn't make sense.

Removing the apron Peggy insisted she wore—though her shabby maternity dress wasn't worth protecting, and she didn't have anything more suitable to wear because when half-heartedly packing before coming here she'd expected to be taken home on discharge from the clinic—she stated, 'I've been idling around for far too long in the lap of luxury. I must go home and help them through this.'

Her parents would be feeling gutted at the prospect of losing Rylands—her father rightly blaming himself and her mother loyally blaming everyone else and trying very hard, bless her, not to cry. 'I'll look up train times, then pack.'

Aiming a wobbly smile in Peggy's direction, Anna headed for the stairs. The fully equipped nursery had been the first surprising intimation that she and Sholto were expected to remain at Francesco's London address for a week or two after Arnold and Peggy had collected them from the clinic. How long she would have stayed if she hadn't had that phone call she didn't know. Until Francesco eventually returned, unable to drag herself away until she'd seen him again?

Mounting the stairs, she compressed her soft lips, cross with herself for that unbidden and somehow demeaning thought. She would always remember his kindness, his unstinting support while she had been giving birth, but that didn't mean she wanted to see him again. *Ever*, she stressed firmly as she entered the room set aside as a nursery and bent over her sleeping son, her heart swelling with love. She was unaware that the moment she'd closed the kitchen door behind her Peggy had darted to the phone.

Although it was only early afternoon Anna shifted with impatience on the velvet-upholstered chair she'd dragged to the window of the first-floor sitting room.

Watching for Arnold's return.

'Arnold will drive you to your parents' home.' Peggy had popped her head round the nursery door while Anna had been feeding Sholto. 'He's out on an errand at the moment, so you can have lunch before you set out.'

'Oh—if he doesn't mind…' It would be a great relief to be travelling in the comfort of the spacious Lexus kept for the Powells' use rather than having to carry Sholto and all his attendant impedimenta on public transport. Nevertheless, it seemed an imposition.

'Of course not! It will be his pleasure. Mind you, I'll really miss having you and baby around,' she'd added. Then, 'As soon as you've finished here come down for lunch.'

Lunch, helping Peggy clear up afterwards, and then her packing, had passed the time. But now, waiting, it hung heavily. It would be a wrench to have to end this interlude of comfort and luxury, with no care in the world except the sheer pleasure and joy of looking after her baby.

But it had been only a brief interlude, and harsh reality was calling her back.

There would be so much to do. Smartening Rylands for the sale was a no-go area. They would need an army of unaffordable painters and decorators, gardeners and so on. No, she would have to get her business up and running again. Mum, on her meet-your-new grandson visit, had said she'd be more than happy to babysit while she was working. It would be a terrible wrench to leave him, but it would have to be done. And then, of course, she'd have to help find somewhere cheap to rent for them to live—

The sound of a car drawing to a halt below had her on her feet. Expecting Arnold, she felt her heart jerk painfully when she looked down and saw Francesco swing smoothly out of the Ferrari.

Leaping back from the window, Anna put her hand to her breast, where her heart was behaving as if she'd just run a double marathon. Her knees were shaky as she headed across the room. She hated the way he could still affect her—hated him for the way he had lied to her, used her body, shattered her confidence and broken her heart.

Reminding herself that there was nothing between them now but that maintenance contract, sternly telling herself she'd moved on, she opened the door and stepped out onto the soft carpeting of the hushed first-floor corridor, determined to go down and politely explain that she and Sholto would be leaving as soon as Arnold returned. Thank him—but not too fulsomely—for his hospitality.

But he was ahead of her—literally. She watched his broad, elegantly suited back disappear into the nursery next to the bedroom she'd been given. After a sharp intake of breath she followed, and emotional turmoil welled up inside her as she saw him standing over the crib, one hand going out to gently touch the sleeping baby's velvety cheek.

She should be there, at his side. Both of them adoring this precious life they'd created between them, secure in their commitment to each other, their love, their future together. For a bleak moment she felt helplessly excluded.

It wasn't like that. It never could be. They weren't a real family unit, she reminded herself on a spurt of anger. He might find his baby son a transient novelty, but as far as he was concerned his son's mother was just one in a line of discarded bedmates. She was surprised he'd even remembered her name!

'Don't worry—I won't be sponging on your charity much longer. I'll be out of your hair just as soon as Arnold turns up!' The words were low, full of anger, and she didn't know where they'd come from. Propelled from deep inside her on an unstoppable surge of emotional chaos, a light year away from the polite and dignified leavetaking she'd meant to deliver.

Slowly, Francesco straightened, turned. His eyes, she noted uncaringly, were like chips of ice, his lean face was hard, his beautiful mouth stark. So she was being rude and objectionable, as he'd labeled. Something he wouldn't stand for in anyone, and certainly not in an ex-lover he'd discarded like so much trash! So what did she care?

Every nerve-end bristling, she walked further into the room. Mindful of the need not to wake the baby, her words were low but as haughty as she could make them. 'Close the door on your way out. And let me know when Arnold gets back.'

She might have known! One stride brought him to her side. His hand was on her arm and she was with him, out of the door in the time it took to flick an eyelash.

'You don't tell me what to do!' His words stung her as he closed the nursery door quietly behind them. 'From now on I call the shots. I advise you to accept that with grace. Otherwise you will suffer the consequences of my displeasure.'

'I'm shaking already!' she sniped, trying to get her breath back, trying to wrest her arm free of his punitive grip and failing. 'Only remember,' she flung at him as he frog-marched her back into the sitting room, 'I'll be gone as soon as Arnold gets back, so you'll be "calling the shots", as you put it, to thin air!'

'Compose yourself.' He steered her towards the chintz-covered sofa. 'I have something to say to you regarding your future. And my son's.'

What? Suddenly dreadfully nervous, she sat, her mind frantically worrying over what was going on in his mind. She watched him as he was watching her, his savagely handsome features unreadable.

He'd said 'my son', and she'd seen how he'd looked at little Sholto as he'd slept only a few minutes ago, remembering how, during that short time he'd spent with them in the clinic and when he'd insisted on choosing a name, how he had held the tiny shawl-wrapped bundle so tenderly.

Ice clamped her heart. Did he mean to take her baby from her? He couldn't do that, could he? She wouldn't let him! Sounding tougher than she felt, she swept her hair out of her eyes with one hand and lashed, 'Spit it out, then! As soon as Arnold gets here, I'm off. With Sholto,' she stressed.

Francesco held up a lean hand to silence her, and her generously curving mouth closed instinctively while an unwelcome twist of nervous excitement wriggled inside her. She watched dark colour steal over his prominent cheekbones when his eyes, drawn to her mouth, stayed there until, his own mouth suddenly tightening, he stated harshly, 'Peggy phoned me to tell me you were leaving. Arnold won't be taking you anywhere—I suggested he take the opportunity to visit his brother.'

'Then we'll get a train!' Anna said thinly, absorbing that bombshell, deeply hurt because Peggy had fooled her, gone behind her back, lied about Arnold driving her. During her time here she'd really believed the older woman was her friend.

So the train it would have to be. She wouldn't dream of asking her father to fetch her in her van. The state it was in, it probably wouldn't do the distance. Besides, he drove like a lunatic, his head in the clouds. But…

'Nick will collect us!' Why hadn't she thought of him before? He'd do anything for her; he'd always said so.

Leaping to her feet, not looking at Francesco, she started for the door, but his tall frame came between her and her objective, strong hands on her shoulders, staying her.

'You are going nowhere. So you can forget your knight in shining armour,' he stated icily. 'And don't blame Peggy. I've had to be away, but I instructed her to let me know if you showed signs of leaving with my son, and to keep you here until I managed to get back. Fortunately I'd just arrived back from Italy for a board meeting at the London office.'

For a moment their eyes clashed. Hers stormy green, his steel. His words weren't making sense, because physical response flared through her at his touch. Her breath caught in her throat and tears of shame stung the backs of her eyes. She knew what a louse he was beneath that sensationally attractive exterior, so why was he able, with one touch, to make her feel so desperately needy? Needy for him.

She should be immune to all that raw sexuality. Despising herself because she wasn't, she pushed out thickly, 'Why?'

The moment the question was out she knew it was redundant. She knew why. He wanted Sholto. Everything pointed to it. Gently, he pushed her unresisting body back onto the sofa and joined her, angling his virile frame into the corner. Watching her.

Her spine slumping, Anna tried to will away the wave

of weakness that was now swamping her. What would he do? Offer her money to relinquish all rights to her baby? Hire a team of hotshot lawyers to gain custody through the courts if she refused—as she would?

She wouldn't let him! She would fight for her baby until the last breath left her body, she vowed, hysteria rising. Because she knew he was ruthless, an arch manipulator, with the vast financial backing to get what he wanted.

Apprehension ripped through her as she waited for an answer. And waited. Until, on the point of screaming, she risked a direct look.

Emotionless silver eyes looked back at her. One dark brow rose with insulting indolence as he drawled, 'Tantrum over? Willing to listen?'

As unwilling as it was possible to be! But the sooner she knew his intentions the more time she'd have to work out how to fight him. Her hands shook. She twisted her fingers together, not wanting him to see how nervous she was. Her face pale, she nodded.

'I shall marry you.'

Anna's breath snagged in her throat. She caught her lower lip between her teeth, nipping to convince herself she wasn't dreaming. A statement so blandly spoken he might as well have announced that he was going to get a haircut!

She would have laughed in his face if she hadn't felt like crying. It hurt so very much. How often on the island, when he'd assured her he loved her, had she yearned, hoped, believed she would hear those words from him? Lowering her head, hiding behind her untamed mane of hair, she struggled to contain her emotions for long enough to tell him no.

Watching her, watching her colour come and go, the way she hid behind her glorious hair, Francesco twisted his sensual mouth bitterly. Once that proposal had been burning his tongue, the ring burning a hole in his breast pocket, its pale yellow diamond chosen because it had reminded him of her hair. But a few ill-timed words from her hare-brained loser of a father had had him savagely cutting her out of his life, reminded that all women were the same—not to be trusted when a man's wealth and status were dangled in front of their scheming eyes.

And now he was doing what he'd vowed—post-Anna—he would never do. He was asking a woman to marry him.

But it was necessary.

Discovering in himself an unsuspected depth of devotion when he'd first laid eyes on his son, he knew he could never cut him out of his life.

'I want my son.' He voiced his thoughts aloud into the silence, his voice husky with need. 'Ideally, a child needs both parents. Permanently. I had thought it would be enough for me to do the responsible thing and provide financial support. Since holding him I find that it is far from enough. Hence—' harshness now cloaked his words '—the need for us to marry. Because, naturally, he will need his mother, too.'

Still in shock, Anna got out unevenly, 'No. I won't. I couldn't bear it!'

'Such protestations don't cut any ice with me,' Francesco drawled. 'Marriage to wealth was what you aimed for, so why bore me with spurious denials now?'

She did look at him then, green eyes flashing outrage. When she'd wanted to spend the rest of her life with him, had loved him so very much she'd felt she couldn't live without him, she hadn't known he was wealthy beyond the dreams of avarice! Now she knew—and she knew other things too.

'You don't love me—you don't love anyone but yourself,' she gasped, feeling colour flood her face, unprepared for the quietly spoken statement that turned her blood to ice.

'I love my son.'

'We don't have to marry,' she got out before sheer terror could claim her.

Marriage would mean sharing his bed, giving him rights over her body. It would destroy her! She knew herself far too well. Sharing the intimacies of marriage with him, she would go back to being besotted. His shattering sexual attraction was her nemesis—because not even knowing what a heartless bastard he was could cure her of that demeaning weakness.

'If you really want to, you could see him whenever you wanted. I wouldn't stop you,' she offered in desperation.

He was looking at her with disturbing indifference, as if her offer was beneath his notice. Anna shivered and dredged up an argument that would hold water. 'It would never work—marriage, I mean. How could it? We don't love each other, and we both know you'd soon be out of my bed and into one occupied by one of those glitzy model-types you seem to favour. I do read the papers, so I know you do that macho stuff, and are rarely seen without the necessary arm candy!' she huffed. 'We'd end

up fighting, hating each other, and I'd start throwing things
and you'd probably throw them back—just think what
damage that kind of marriage would do to little Sholto!'

She'd made her point—surely she had? she agonised.

But he shot her a look of what she could only describe
as amused contempt as he countered, 'I wouldn't *be* in
your bed. My needs in that department can be easily
catered to.' Though he hadn't been remotely interested
since— But he wasn't going to dwell on that.

And he would want to be in her bed, he derided himself
with painful honesty. The first time he'd laid eyes on her
he'd been tempted, had spent the whole of that first night
fantasising about losing himself in that sensationally lush
body. And the reality had been beautiful beyond his
dreams, putting his fantasies into deep shade.

But he would make sure he was never tempted again.
He was strong enough. Hadn't his character been
likened to steel? 'Our marriage will be on paper only. A
façade to provide our son with two parents.' A frown
clefted his brow, his sculpted features hard. 'Immediately after the ceremony—civil, naturally—we will go
to my family home in Tuscany, where my son will grow
up with the freedom and happiness he needs. He will
have the uncomplicated childhood I never enjoyed. You,
as his mother, will share my wealth and my status, enjoy
the respect that that will bring, and in return you will
never complain. Should you attempt to remove my son
from my protection, or take a lover, you will be history.'

Raw anger flicked deep inside her. It took gold-plated
heartless arrogance to lay down such punitive rules.
Colour staining her cheeks, heightening the brilliance of

her eyes, she flung at him, 'So I'm to live like a nun in a gilded cage, far away from family and friends? No, thanks. I don't rate feather-bedding that highly!'

'You like money—you like sex. But you can't have both. Get used to it.' His cold intonation fuelled her anger. Who did he think he was?

She got to her feet, unable to sit still a moment longer. 'On Ischia I thought you were the most wonderful, exciting, caring man ever to breathe—now I know you're the dregs!' she told him stormily. 'I won't marry you, and I withdraw the offer to allow you access. Ever! I won't have my son contaminated!'

'Sit down.' Lean fingers fastened around her wrist, tugging her back beside him. Steely grey eyes set a collision course with hers, and her breath came feebly even though her heart was clattering like a runaway train. The force of his personality scared her silly, but she held his gaze, not willing to let him see her weakness.

'You have a regrettable tendency to behave like a drama queen,' he incised, his devastating features set in grim lines. 'You once set your sights on my wealth—you can't deny it. Now it is yours for the taking I suggest you stop behaving like a spoiled brat and face the fact that you can't have me twisted round your pretty fingers, doting putty in your hands. Accept it. Or tell me what you do want from our marriage and I will consider it.'

Anna clamped her mouth shut. What she wanted—would have wanted when she'd thought the sun rose and set with him—she could never have. But she wasn't telling him that. And as for denying that she wanted to get her hands on his wretched money, forget it! Let him think what he liked. She wasn't going to lay her already bleeding heart at his feet and confess that all she'd ever wanted was his love.

'Nothing to say? I thought not.' He dealt her a brooding look from smoky eyes. 'Then I will lay the full details of my proposal in front you of, and you can decide which road you wish to travel.'

Anna stared back at him, twisting her hands on her lap, dry-mouthed with tension as she wondered what he was going to come out with next. If she didn't know better she would have sworn on oath that this wasn't the same man as the exciting, laid-back charmer she'd fallen in love with on Ischia. Talk about Jekyll and Hyde!

'First option: we marry—with the stipulations already spoken of. Furthermore, I have had your father's situation examined, and find he is about to lose your mother her family home.' He leaned back, his eyes contemptuous. 'If we marry I will clear his debts and provide him with employment within one of my companies to help him curb his…shall we say…eccentricities? And that must not be considered an inducement—or a philanthropic gesture on my behalf,' he drawled with cynicism. 'It would not be good for my image were it to become known that my parents-in-law were penniless and homeless.'

She wanted to hit him. 'I hate you!' she said thickly. He obviously looked on her and her family as being beneath contempt—lesser beings who would fall in with his dictates with humiliating gratitude.

Ignoring her interjection, Francesco continued, almost purring now. 'If, however, you refuse my proposal, then

I promise you I will take my son from you. Legally. And don't think that wouldn't happen. It would.'

He got to his feet with the fluid grace that had once mesmerised her. 'I'll leave you to think it over.' Shooting his cuff, he glanced at the face of the slim gold watch that banded his wrist. 'You have an hour to reach a decision.'

CHAPTER SEVEN

SHE'D said she would marry him.

A bad decision? The worst one possible from her point of view! But what choice did she have?

Refuse, as every instinct she possessed counselled, and she'd see her parents lose their home and their dignity. Dad struggling to cope with a job that was far more suitable for a much younger man. Mum mourning the loss of the house that had been in her family for generations and trying not to show it. And she'd have to live with the knowledge that she could have prevented it, all the time having the dark threat of Francesco gaining sole custody of her precious little son hanging over her head, with the totally chilling knowledge that with the help of clever lawyers and a bottomless pit of money he'd do exactly that.

So. No choice at all.

Now, almost twenty-four hours following her graceless acceptance, she remembered Francesco's chilly, 'A wise decision,' and the way his dark head had dipped in terse acknowledgement before he'd swung on his heels and left the room, leaving her struggling to come to terms with what the future held.

Sitting out on the terrace in the late-afternoon sunshine, with her baby on her lap, she remembered, too, waking this morning, before the baby alarm could alert her to the raucous fact that Sholto was ready for his early feed, padding to the nursery and finding Francesco already there, giving his son his bottle.

Resentment that he had denied her the only pleasure now left to her—caring for her baby—had warred with the proof that he meant to be a devoted hands-on father. She'd crept back to her room and hadn't set eyes on him since.

On her lap, Sholto kicked his legs and gurgled, and Anna's heart turned over, bursting with love. In agreeing to a loveless marriage she was doing the right thing. For Sholto and her parents, at least.

Her baby would grow up with all the advantages she, alone, could never hope to provide, secure in the love of both parents. And she would never, *never* give him the slightest hint that his parents' marriage was nothing but an empty sham, that hatred and mistrust lay beneath the smooth surface. Surely it was a price worth paying?

Pausing at the head of the terrace, Francesco felt his heart jolt against his breastbone. He had never seen anything so beautiful. Mother and child in the dappled shade of the overhanging false acacia, her body curved protectively over the gurgling infant.

A beautiful enigma. An innocent, or a clever schemer? Since this afternoon's conversation with his lawyer nothing was quite as clear-cut as it had been.

Intent on giving instructions for a watertight prenuptial agreement, he'd been stunned when the older man had imparted that his bride-to-be had refused to sign the now redundant maintenance contract until the amount stated had been significantly reduced—pared down until it provided just the bare essentials.

The lawyer had excused his lack of communication on the subject. Passing on that information hadn't seemed necessary. If the young lady in question had held out for a larger amount—well, that, of course, would have been very different. His client's instructions on the matter would have been sought at once.

So what was going on? Francesco's brow clenched as he watched his small son grab a fistful of that glorious hair. He had never believed her when she'd protested that she didn't want anything from him, dismissing it as so much bluster and hot air, cloaking her desire to squeeze as much as she could from him, or a forlorn attempt to convince him that when she'd vowed she loved him back on the island, she'd had no knowledge of who he really was. Which didn't hold water. Hadn't she let slip, only yesterday, that she'd seen articles about him—and one of his latest lovers—in the press?

He hadn't been seen with a female since her father— on her advice?—had jumped right in, giving the impression that he recognised him from the financial papers and asking for a huge chunk of investment in some scheme or other. In his book it was clear that she'd lied about not being aware of his financial status.

So what was her long game? Pretend to be uninterested in his wealth—even to the extent of having that contract altered, knowing he would get to hear of it— while all the time banking on the astute belief that having seen his child, held him, he wouldn't want to let him go and would offer a form of marriage as the smoothest way forward? Giving her access to everything that was his.

Clever!

Cynicism bracketing his mouth now, he strode forward, gently scooping his son from her lap, ignoring her startled intake of breath. 'I'll take him. There are people waiting to see you. In your room.'

'People? Who?' The shock of his sudden appearance left her open-mouthed, her breath gone because he was so spectacularly handsome he made her feel dizzy.

Not deigning to answer, he laid a beautifully crafted hand on his son's tummy. '*Ciao, bambino!* Soon, when your tiny feet grow bigger, Papa will teach you to play football—the next day it will be chess!'

Despite herself, and the acid sense of exclusion, Anna felt her mouth quirk. Mental pictures of a large man and a tiny dark-haired boy kicking a ball about in an imagined Tuscan flower-strewn meadow brought a soft sheen of wistfulness to her eyes.

Venting a tiny sigh, because she wanted to stay, be included in the father and son bonding session, she rose, smoothed down her shabby old maternity dress and set out to find out for herself who the people were.

She'd just about gained the garden door at the head of the terrace when Francesco remarked, 'By the way, I visited your parents earlier. They were delighted by the news of our marriage, and almost hysterical when they heard that their debts will be cleared. I got out before I could be drowned in tears of gratitude.'

Anna's steps faltered only a moment on receipt of that flatly delivered statement, then she surged on. She didn't turn to look at him, to acknowledge that she'd heard what he'd said. Her face was flaming with humiliation, and she didn't want him to see her monumental discomfiture and gloat.

He'd sounded dismissive, bored. As if she and her parents were contemptible. Well, what did she expect? He'd said his seemingly mega-generous offer to clear their debts was being made to protect his own precious image—certainly not an altruistic gesture to get a couple of good if slightly eccentric people out of the huge hole they'd dug for themselves.

Trying to put him out of her mind and concentrate on the possible identity of her mystery visitors—Mum and Dad, perhaps?—she swiftly mounted the stairs, headed for her room, pushed open the door and was confronted by two strange women.

Painfully smart women, surrounded by a sea of classy-looking boxes. The older of the two, with the dark hair scraped so tightly back it looked painted on, rose from the chair she'd been occupying.

'Miss Maybury?' Dark eyes swept over her, and Anna could have sworn she heard a wince in her voice. 'Signor Mastroianni instructed us to bring suitable clothes for you to try.'

A slight accent. French? Anna's arched brows drew together. More charity? She didn't want it.

'I'm sorry—you've wasted your time,' she said stiffly, half choking on this new mortification. 'I don't need new clothes.'

A pencil-thin eyebrow rose in repudiation of that mistaken opinion. 'The *signor* was most insistent.'

'No.' She had stuff of her own back at Rylands. Someone could fetch it. She might be a kept woman— courtesy of darling little Sholto—but she didn't aim to look like one. Stepping back, moving as if to show her visitors the door, she saw a look of stark apprehension flicker across the enamelled-looking face, and her soft heart immediately capitulated.

The side of Francesco's character she hadn't dreamt existed when they'd said their passionate farewells on Ischia had told her that anyone who failed to deliver on instruction was in for a tough time. The uneviable situation she found herself in wasn't this woman's fault, so why should she suffer?

So, 'OK. I'll try one or two things.' She felt gratifyingly vindicated for her *volte-face* when both women visibly relaxed, smiling, practically purring, as tops were pulled away from boxes, layers of tissue reverently parted, to reveal costly fabrics in a rainbow of gorgeous colours.

After all, it might be fun to try on the type of designer gear she'd only previously glimpsed on the glossy pages of swanky magazines. And Francesco could buy the lot, but that didn't mean she would ever wear them.

Removing her dress under the pained eyes of the women—maybe they didn't rate chainstore undies?— Anna stamped on the ignoble thought that she would be more than glad to see the back of the maternity tents she'd lived in for what felt like for ever and gradually, very gradually, began to enjoy herself.

Partly because the women made highly flattering

remarks—which no way did Anna take seriously—and partly because she adored the way pure silk, cashmere and linen felt against her body, she went along with what she saw as an amusing game quite willingly. Only blushing furiously when the older of the two, her head on one side, one eyebrow raised to an impossible height remarked, 'The *signor*, he knows the details of your measurements perfectly!'

Intimately! He knew her body so intimately! Her tummy quivered, heat pooling where it shouldn't. She deplored it. She wasn't going to go there!

And suddenly it wasn't fun any more. Her mouth set, she reached for the one remaining garment box. Get it over with. Her eyes sparking with irritation now, over this senseless waste of time, she stood like a wooden doll while the older woman zipped her up and the younger folded away the lovely caramel-coloured linen suit and creamy camisole she'd just stepped out of.

'*Très belle*—look—' Hands on Anna's shoulders turned her towards the pier glass, and her stormy eyes widened as she viewed a self that looked totally unlike herself.

The finest black silk dress moulded her voluptuous breasts, skimmed her back-to-normal tiny waist, caressed the sensuous curve of her hips, then floated down to narrow ankles that just cried out for the high-heeled glittery strappy shoes the younger woman was advancing with. Somehow, her widened eyes registered, the sombre colour made the naked skin of her arms, upper breast and shoulders look like whipped cream and her hair like glossy coils of platinum.

Sexy siren!

It wasn't her—not her at all!

Her cheeks pinkening, adding extra glitter to her stormy green eyes, she was in haste to remove the dress. But the ultra-fine concealed zip was beyond the efforts of her fumbling fingers and turning, looking for assistance, she froze on the spot as Francesco walked in as if he owned the place. Which he did, of course, she grumped at herself.

She swallowed a ragged intake of breath as she found herself unable to look away from his lean, bronzed, classically Italian features, from the searing impact of slightly narrowed eyes that had darkened to unreadable charcoal pools, or the way even in well-worn jeans and a sleeveless black vest he exuded class, natural sophistication and the shattering good-looks that top-flight movie stars would envy.

He was irresistible on an entirely primitive level, she thought despairingly, appalled by her weakness, by her contrariness in lusting after the one man in the world she absolutely hated.

His eyes on Anna, Francesco strode further into the room, his accent more marked than usual as he instructed, 'Madame Laroche, would you and your assistant wait downstairs? My housekeeper will bring coffee. I will join you shortly.'

Periphery movement, smiles and bobbing heads. Anna didn't even note when the women left the room. Francesco was advancing towards her, and she could concentrate on nothing else. There was tension in every line of his unforgettable features, something almost pagan smouldering in his eyes as they swept her, the sexy siren personna that wasn't her at all.

Or was it?

Anna's head spun. It was difficult to breathe and she couldn't think straight—not while there was that wicked throb deep inside her. She trembled, something far too responsive to this devil's erotic magnetism trickling down her spine.

'Madame Laroche chose well.' A scant twelve inches away, he stopped. He was having trouble with his breathing. That dress clung to every lethally voluptuous inch of her body, and the mass of bright hair was inviting him to touch, to run his fingers through the silky coils. His voice thickened. 'That dress is dynamite.'

Anna's insides squirmed. On its own the dress was discreetly revealing, classy. But with her embarrassingly aroused body inside it, it was shocking. She crossed her arms over her chest to hide the way her breasts were straining to escape over the top of the low-cut bodice, as if the fine fabric couldn't contain such bounty. Her nipples were tellingly prominent.

Her voice scratchy with her attempts to control her wretched body's seemingly automatic response to this one man, she pushed at him, 'She can take it all back. You'll waste your money if you buy any of it. I won't wear it!'

'Why not?' Unfazed, he fastened his eyes on the soft fullness of her mouth, and had the forbidden memory of exactly how that mouth had felt in the possession of his, the generous, unquestioning response that had never failed to drive him crazy. He felt his body harden and knew this couldn't go on.

'Because you only want me to wear stuff like this so you aren't ashamed of me—just like you'd hate for anyone to know that your in-laws are sleeping in card-board boxes—no good for your precious image!'

She slung the reminder at him and rejoiced to see his flush of discomfiture. It lasted a bare second before he countered, with enviable cool, 'No. That is not the case. It would give me pleasure to see the mother of my son wearing lovely things.'

'And I'm supposed to care about your pleasure?' Anna's brows almost hit her hairline. The sheer gall of the man! He had used her and discarded her, and he obviously despised her family—and her. He wouldn't be giving her the time of day if he hadn't dis-covered he was to be a father. And as sure as night followed day he wouldn't have proposed marriage if he hadn't fallen in love with his son! And yet he expected her to dress in outfits that would give him pleasure! 'I'd rather give you a black eye!' she said, with feeling.

'I don't think so,' Francesco came back with awesome smoothness. 'In fact, there's been a change of plan.'

It took a moment for Anna's seething brain to calm down enough to take that in. 'In what way?' He could only mean he'd rethought the marriage stuff, come to his senses. And that shouldn't make her feel strangely bereft, with the humiliating recognition that she really must have been totally missing from the queue when brains were handed out, but she did feel ridiculously bereft.

'Our marriage is to be a real one.'

Colour flooded her face at that statement. Her arms,

still crossed over her chest, jerked, her fingernails biting into the flesh of her shoulders.

'I find I still want your body,' he confessed, with just a hint of self-derision.

'It's only this dress,' she mumbled, hiding her blushes behind her hair at the crazy thought of being his sex slave, knowing, to her utter shame, that his sexual magnetism could make her do anything he wanted her to do.

'No, it's not,' Francesco said thickly, not telling her he'd still thought her the most beautiful thing he'd ever seen earlier, even dressed in that awful tent thing. Lust, of course. Knowing what he now knew of her, it could be nothing else. 'I've changed my mind about going through simply a form of marriage. It would be—' under her widened gaze he sought an apposite word, felt his heart lurch, and supplied '—uncomfortable. A full marriage would make life easier for both of us.'

Initially he'd thought that having his son would be enough. That he could concentrate on his son and as good as ignore her existence except when necessity— social or business—meant they had to appear as a couple. But being driven half out of his mind by unsatisfied lust, knowing from past experience that he could make her burn with the same desire that burned in him, would make a paper marriage untenable. Ultimately harming his son.

Pent-up emotion had her shaking like a leaf and she stammered, 'S…sex. You mean you'd expect me to have sex with you? You'd—you'd think you'd paid for it!' Her voice rose by several decibels. 'I'd feel like a prostitute!'

'Calmare—' He reached for her but she backed away,

arms still crossed protectively over her breasts. He sucked in his breath. *Dio mio!* It would not be like that! He'd had affairs in the past, before he met her, and had been up-front about sex. Beautiful women who knew not to expect anything approaching a long-term commitment, who retired discreetly from the scene with some lavish parting gift when his interest faded.

But with Anna it wouldn't be like that. It was a mystery he wasn't in the mood to try to solve. He only knew. 'It wouldn't be like that,' he verbalised gruffly, then consciously smoothed away an uncharacteristic feeling of walking on quicksand. He advanced until she'd backed herself against a wall. 'We'll have a proper wedding—no downbeat civil service—and our marriage will be consummated.' His voice thickened as he put his hands over hers and drew them slowly down to her sides. 'Whatever our differences, you can't have forgotten how good we once were together.'

How could she ever forget? Anna thought wildly, the intensity of her emotions making her feel spaced out. His eyes slowly travelled her quivering body. Alarm bells were ringing in her head but she couldn't look away.

Her eyes were riveted to the slow smile that curved his sensual mouth as he told her, 'It will be good for us again, I promise.' His hands slid up to her shoulders, detouring tantalisingly over her engorged breasts. She swallowed convulsively. She felt boneless, something hot clenching inside as he imparted huskily, 'Why live in agony through the years of our marriage? Why deny ourselves the release we can give each other?'

'Just sex,' she got out, still trying to fight a battle she

knew she was losing. She wanted him and she couldn't deny that truth. Back on Ischia she had become addicted to him, and he was proving to be an impossible habit to kick.

'Don't knock it!' Smooth as cream, he lowered his dark head and took her mouth with a sensual expertise that made her whimper, whimper some more, then melt and cling to his broad shoulders for support.

Not thinking of what she was doing, not capable of a single rational thought, Anna wriggled her body closer into the hard length of his, felt his deep, responsive shudder as his mouth plundered hers with fierce male urgency. He pressed her back against the wall, firm hands shaping her eager body, the curve of her hips, the mound at the base of her tummy and up to her tingling breasts, long fingers slipping beneath the silky neckline making her gasp with wanton pleasure, wrench her mouth from his and fling her head back in a blatant invitation which he took.

Easing the straps away, he slid the silk from her breasts, dark colour a flash along his angular cheekbones, his eyes heavily lidded as he bent to close his mouth round each taut nipple in turn. Gasping, she dug her fingers into the solid muscle of his shoulders and reality, already a hazy distant thing, slipped entirely away. She was lost again, his again, and her body was screaming demands that only he could meet.

'You are convinced?' He drew away, ran long fingers through his rumpled hair. 'I have proved how good we are together, *si*? Our marriage will be no hardship.' He dealt her a smile that drove the breath out of her lungs before turning. 'Madame Laroche waits. Wear something that will give me pleasure when we dine tonight.'

As the door closed behind him Anna wrapped her arms around her treacherous, unsated body and vented a long, shuddering sob. In his hands she was putty, to be moulded as he pleased. He could seduce her with a look, render her powerless.

He had just proved it. And there was no way out of a marriage that would be full of hot sex and empty of love—not if she wanted to keep her son.

CHAPTER EIGHT

'SOPHIA will arrive on the company jet later this afternoon. Arnold will meet her, and she should be in time to join us for dinner.'

'Sophia?' Anna prompted after a beat of silence. Francesco's statement had been delivered with the first sign of enthusiasm he'd shown all morning.

His sensual mouth was flat, but his dark eyes brooded as they finally turned to her. Had the charade over and done with only a scant five minutes ago brought home with a sickening crunch the reality of the situation they found themselves in?

In the ground-floor drawing room, surrounded by screamingly expensive and beautiful antiques and paintings, Francesco had invited her to make her selection from the fabulous rings displayed in a briefcase that had arrived chained to the wrist of a tall, thin male who looked more like an undertaker than a purveyor of fine gems, accompanied by a hovering stone-faced, flint-eyed bodyguard.

Beneath three pairs of increasingly impatient eyes Anna had only been able to stare at the dazzling array as long awkward moments passed, her throat tightening with every uncomfortable second. She'd felt like an actor who had forgotten her lines and who, if she remembered them, would be reluctant to speak them.

In the end it had been Francesco who had plucked a flashy diamond cluster from its velvet nest without ceremony, and settled it on the third finger of her left hand with about as much romance as a guy would show stuffing loose change back in his pocket.

'My sister,' he now answered on a bite. 'She is flying from Rome and will stay until the wedding to assist you.'

'I didn't know you had a sister.' Anna raised questioning green eyes. She realized she knew very little about him really. Only that he was filthy rich and a womanizer, who liked just now and then to amuse himself by pretending to be dirt-poor and seducing gullible little virgins who wouldn't get ideas about his wealth because he made sure they stayed ignorant. Recalling the cheap brass chain he'd worn the first time she'd set eyes on him, she nearly exploded with the desire to jump up and hit him.

But negative backwards-looking emotions wouldn't get her anywhere in the situation that had been as good as thrust upon her. She took a deep steadying breath and invited, 'Tell me about her.'

Anna's small hands fisted against the pale cotton of the smoothly styled culottes she'd teamed with an emerald camisole top—both garments courtesy of Madame Laroche's good taste and Francesco's bottomless bank account—and did her best to push the other known fact—that he was probably the sexiest guy to walk the planet—right to the back of her mind.

Difficult when he levered his lean, power-packed frame out of the small sofa he'd been occupying and stood looking down at her, feet slightly apart, hands in the trouser pockets of the superbly styled dove-grey suit he was wearing.

He was so breathtakingly handsome he made her feel faint. And so damnably in control that he made her feel so churned up she didn't know where she was half the time. Like after that torrid scene in her bedroom yesterday, when he'd announced his intention to make their marriage a real one and proved, to her private shame, that she'd be a complete push-over. She'd expected him to come to her last night. But he hadn't, and that had left her not knowing whether to be mightily relieved or sick as a parrot!

Now he levelled at her, 'I have wedding arrangements to make. Perhaps you might contact your parents and invite them to stay here for a day or two before the ceremony? I'll let you know the date.' And he was gone, leaving her feeling so aggravated she could explode. The diamond cluster on her finger was like a ton weight, dragging her down.

He couldn't have made his intention to refuse her admission to any part of his life or his family's clearer if he'd written in it red letters a mile high! As the mother of his son he would dress her, feed her, house her in luxury, bed her when he felt like it—but he would give her no part of himself.

Setting her delicate jaw, Anna got to her feet. He was determined to shut her out. What she felt wasn't deep hurt—of course not—it was pique, and, piqued, she would do something about it. After all, he didn't love her, and she as sure as hens were toothless didn't love him, so why should she feel unbearably hurt?

She found Peggy in the kitchen, shelling peas. Pulling a chair out, Anna sat at the table, grabbed a handful of pods and said, as lightly as she could, 'So Sophia arrives later today? Francesco was in a hurry, so he didn't have time to put me properly in the picture. What's she like? Older or younger?' Sneaky, or what? But if she was to learn anything at all about the man who was to be her husband and his family she had to use any means at her disposal.

'Oh, you'll like her,' Peggy promised warmly. 'She's married to a rich Italian banker—Fabio Bocelli—but there's no side to her. Come to think of it, she and her big brother are both like that—they treat everybody as equals. It doesn't matter who they are or what they've got, it's the person inside the skin who counts.'

Really? Despite her best efforts to put on a guileless front, Anna felt one brow shoot towards her hairline.

'Anyway—' Peggy pushed herself to her feet. 'I'll make coffee while you finish that lot. Oh!' Colour washed her narrow cheeks. 'Listen to me! You'll soon be the mistress here, and there's me bossing you around like you were a kitchen maid!'

'Don't be daft!' Anna grinned, grabbing a fresh handful of pods. 'We're friends, right? Make that coffee. I'm gasping!' She'd rapidly forgiven Peggy for the way she'd lied to keep her here until Francesco could put in an appearance. When the boss asked, Peggy would oblige—without question. Not out of fear for her position but from loyalty and respect. He must have treated the Powells much better than he'd treated her to gain such unfailing obedience to his slightest wish, she thought sourly.

As she industriously podded the last of the peas, the diamonds on her finger winked coldly. Grimly, Anna slid the ring off and dug it deep into the pocket of her culottes. Wretched spiky thing! If it had been a thin gold band adorned with a single tiny seed pearl but given with love she would have valued it far more highly than this flashy, eye-wateringly expensive bauble given simply because it was the thing to do.

'There we go—' Peggy slid a coffee mug in front of her and sat down, cradling her own mug, prepared to gossip. 'Now—Sophia. She's six years younger than her brother, so that makes her twenty-eight. She's lively, very pretty, and has a six-year-old daughter—Cristina. Mind you, she'll be leaving her behind with her nanny and Signor Bocelli until nearer the wedding.' She smiled wryly. 'There'll be tantrums there—the little scrap just adores her zio Francesco, and he dotes on her, indulges her rotten! I'm not surprised things have turned out as they have. He's besotted with baby Sholto, but you'll have to watch out he doesn't ruin him with spoiling! Spoil the pair of you, is my guess. You should have seen the look on his face when he broke the news of the wedding—cat got the cream wasn't in it!'

Daddy cat got his kitten, Anna brooded a few hours later. She was just a necessary encumbrance. Necessary to his tiny son's happiness and well-being, not *his*.

Never his.

Wandering around the fabulous ground-floor drawing room, plumping cushions, moving a vase of flowers from one table to another, gave her something to do. She had bathed and fed Sholto, played with him, cuddled him, lunched in solitary splendour, taken her dark-haired little son for an airing in the railed gardens at the heart of the elegant square, and now he slept.

Edgy, unable to settle, she was glad of the interruption when Peggy opened the door and announced impressively, 'A gentleman to see you, madam.'

Still grinning at the formal 'madam', Anna's mouth dropped open when Nick ambled in carrying a huge bouquet of startlingly colourful flowers. 'For you.' He thrust them at her. 'Congrats on the baby, by the way.' His cheerful open face was one big blush. 'So, everything's OK? When I called by your place this morning your mum told me your baby's father's going to marry you. You OK about that?' He shifted his feet, glancing around uneasily. 'Judging by this place he's loaded, but money isn't everything. It didn't take much to work out it must have happened while you were on that holiday—the baby, I mean. And, well, he didn't exactly follow up, did he? Not till he found out by accident he was going to be a dad. Does he want to keep the kid? Is that it? Threatening to take him off you if you don't toe the line? Is that the sort of bloke you want to marry? You can tell me the truth.'

That had been a long speech for Nick. Astute, too. Was he remembering how he'd offered to marry her, care for her baby as if it were his own? Was he feeling hurt and somehow denigrated because he'd been turned down in favour, apparently, of a guy who could offer far more materially?

Her suspicion was confirmed when he stated stiffly, 'Soon as I heard about you getting hitched I had to come and tell you that my offer still stands. If we married quickly no court would grant him custody of the kid. You're his mother, and that gives you a head start, and showing that we would give the lad a stable family background would clinch it. You wouldn't have to worry. I can't give you a fancy lifestyle, but I do care about you.'

He looked so earnest that Anna's throat closed up. Regardless of the personal cost, he was offering her a viable way out, and affection for him made her heart swell.

They were like brother and sister. And they'd always looked out for each other. He wasn't in love with her, but he was looking out for her now. And she couldn't bear him to think she regarded his offer of marriage as second-best, not worth considering.

'I know you care for me—we care for each other. But we're not in love with each other, Nick. We've discussed it before, remember?' She took one of his hands and led him to one of the sofas, placed the flowers at the end and sat down. As he joined her she said, 'You'll make some lucky girl a great husband, Nick. But you see I'm in love with Francesco. I fell in love with him within twenty-four hours of meeting him. I want to be his wife.'

Anna's breath stuck in her throat. She'd said that to make her dear friend feel easier about his rejected proposal. But was it true? Her tummy lurched and she stumbled over her next words. 'You—you deserve to fall in love with a girl who feels the same way.'

Any reservations she might have felt about her claim to be in love with the man she was soon to marry disappeared when Nick grinned, his mild blue eyes washed with relief. 'Then you don't need rescuing? You are happy—not being bullied into doing something you don't want to do?'

'Of course not,' Anna mumbled, her mind in knots over the hardening possibility that she *was* still in love with Francesco—had never really stopped loving him. It made the future seem even bleaker. How would she cope? How could she tread through the years ahead loving a man who saw her only as a necessary encumbrance?

But Nick was blushing again, and telling her, his voice gruff, 'Thing is, if you'd needed me I would have—well, you know—married you, like I suggested. And I wouldn't have taken it any further.'

'Taken what further?'

'Well, there's this girl. Melody. We only met a month ago, and—well, it's early days—only I think—' Unable to articulate further, he spread his big hands, his grin wide enough to split his face.

Anna, overwhelmed with affection for this good, uncomplicated man, this lifelong friend who would have swallowed his feelings for this girl Melody and dedicated himself to caring for her and her child had she needed him, flung her arms around him and cried, 'Didn't I tell you the real thing would happen for you one day? I'm so happy for you! If she's the one, don't you dare let her get away!'

'I won't!' Nick got to his feet, pulling her with him. 'Better make tracks. Get the train back.'

'So soon? Peggy could make us some tea,' Anna offered. Her old and valued friend, uncomplicated and steady, was easier to be around than the tricky enigma that was her future husband.

'Thanks, but I'll pass. Now I know you're OK and everything I'll head home, be in time to phone Melody and fix a date for tonight.'

'Then I'll see you out. And Nick?' She smiled up at him as they headed for the hallway. 'I'm really happy for you. Remember to send me an invitation to the wedding!'

'Will do—and that goes for you, too.' His arm went around her, holding her close, and Anna felt tears clog her throat at the thought of her wedding. She would make her vows and, more fool her, would mean them. While Francesco would just go through the motions.

For a moment Anna closed her eyes, blocking tears. When she opened them again Francesco was walking in through the main door they'd been heading for. Tall and strikingly handsome, so elegant, he made Nick in his cheap brown suit look like a peasant, and his voice was dark menace as he observed, 'How touching. But I would prefer not to see my fiancée being pawed by a garage mechanic whose services are not required here.'

Anna's gasp of outrage was smothered by Nick's grinning, 'On my way, mate. Just called in to check if my services *were* required. And as they're not—' He dropped a light kiss on Anna's cheek and headed swiftly for the door, which Francesco was holding ostentatiously open. Obviously fully aware of six feet plus of intimidating, fist-clenching male, he made a rapid exit, leaving a sizzling silence.

'You're jealous!' Anna's amazement made her feel light-headed. Nick must have picked that up too—hence his unstoppable grin, his tongue-in-cheek riposte in the face of the furious male.

She had never, *ever* seen the so arrogantly in control Francesco look so discomfited as he closed the door with unnecessary force then turned to her. 'I? Jealous?' As if such a concept was beyond human imagining.

Dark colour stained his classically moulded cheekbones as she pointed out, 'Then why were you so rude to him?' Only searing jealousy could have made him lose his famous cool urbanity, and the implications of that made her bones go weak.

His handsome mouth hardened, but there was a febrile glitter in his charcoal-dark eyes as Anna went on, 'The poor guy only called by to say hello and bring me flowers,' knowing that would further rattle his cage. Because Francesco didn't do romantic gestures. Except for when she had first met him, when he had picked wild flowers and tucked them in her hair. But she rapidly thrust that memory aside, concentrating only on the here and now.

'The *poor guy*—' he parodied her tone '—was lucky not to have his jaw broken.' His body tensed and burned at the recollection of wanting to tear the other man limb from limb, because looking at her, at that glorious hair framing her flushed features, that lethally luscious body clothed in silky tones of green that brought out the emerald depths of her lovely eyes, confirmed what he already knew. That no man could look at her and not want to bed her.

'You are to be my wife. You are the mother of my

child,' Francesco pointed out with suppressed fury. 'I take exception to coming home and finding my future wife and some oaf wrapped around each other.'

He caught her raised hand before it could connect, and received an irate shriek. 'Nick is not an oaf! You horrible snob! He's the nicest, kindest friend anyone could have—he's worth a dozen of you!'

'How many times have you slept with him?' he enquired with crushing cool, his eyes like daggers of ice.

'Never!' Anna tried, and failed, to release her wrist from his punitive grasp. 'I don't sleep around—I was a virgin when we met—you know that!'

'And later? After we split?' He was breathing raggedly, suppressing the wave of lust that always washed over him around her, forcing him to voice the cynical doubts that plagued him. 'When you discovered you were pregnant, perhaps? Did you get him on your hook as back-up, in case any plans you might have had to present me with a flesh-and-blood child and demand a handsome settlement from me failed?'

Anna paled. She didn't know how she could still love him, but she did. And he thought she was a scheming monster. The future was a nightmare. Tears she couldn't fight glittered in her eyes, and her voice was thin as she protested, 'How could you think that of me?'

'It's not something that fills me with joy,' he gritted, frowning as his gaze hit her wobbling mouth. 'But I have to face facts. You discovered my private beach, draped yourself alluringly, and waited until I showed up—hoping I'd find you as irresistible as indeed I did.'

So that was what he'd decided, and he was sticking

to it. Nothing she said would make him change his mind. Her slim shoulders shook as tears fell.

Shock made her gasp as, uttering a low expletive, he scooped her up into his arms. 'I can't bear to see you cry. There's no need.'

There was *every* need! Beyond explaining her horrible inner turmoil, Anna sagged in his arms as he carried her upstairs, not even breathless as he told her with infuriating complacency, 'You shouldn't make scenes. They upset you.'

To counter that he had started it would be too childish for words, so she kept her mouth shut. His arrogance, his conviction that he was never in the wrong, inexplicably made her want to giggle—but all desire to give way to hysterical hilarity vanished when he shouldered her bedroom door shut behind them and lowered her to her feet, down the length of his taut, beautifully made body, his hands still holding her against him.

Her tummy muscles tightened. Heat pooled deep inside her. She could feel his arousal. Her breath caught as he used the pads of his thumbs to stroke away the signs of recent tears, and she was powerless to stop the urgent peaking of her breasts against the thin fabric of her camisole top. And he registered the invitation—of course he did—and his hands lifted to tangle in her hair as he took possession of her lush mouth. She gave herself up to sweetly intense sensation, desperate for him as she always would be, she recognised weakly as a stormy river of response raged through her.

Breaking the kiss, Francesco held her eyes as his supple hands dropped to shape her bountiful breasts. He felt her quiver as she wound slender arms around his neck, nuzzling her pelvis into the hardness of his, and he knew he had a monumental fight on his hands.

A fight with himself and with the torrent of male need that told him they were only paces from the bed, murmured far too temptingly that a few deft movements were all that were needed to remove the thin silky fabric that clothed her to-die-for body, scarcely more to jettison his own constricting garments and, lie with her, flesh to eager flesh, skin to burning skin. A fight against the conventional necessities that awaited him.

His breath scorching his lungs, he ground out huskily, 'You want me; I want you. We must put the past way behind us and for Sholto's sake make our marriage work. Be civilised, build on what we have.'

'You mean sex,' Anna whimpered, trembling with need, ravaged by knowing that all he wanted from her was a civilised front and animal lust in the marriage bed. She wanted so much more, but was besotted enough to settle for what she could get.

'What else?' To her shamed humiliation his hand dipped to the waistband of the culottes and dealt with the buttons with a practised ease that excited and further shamed her, dipping his fingers and languourously exploring the slickness between her thighs. 'Don't knock it. Apart from our son, it is all we have.' Silvery eyes mocked her. 'And it is good. Admit it.'

He released her. 'To my regret, I am unable to give the decisive demonstration.' He straightened his wide shoulders. 'Sophia will be arriving at any moment. I must greet her. You will meet at dinner.'

And he was gone in a handful of smooth strides, leaving Anna to wrap her arms around her tormented body and wish she'd never set eyes on him.

He would have his son and heir—with her thrown in as a bonus. A sex slave. A *willing* sex slave, she admitted with an inner cringe of shame. He lusted after her. But lust died. And when it did he would satisfy his needs elsewhere.

She didn't know how she would cope with that!

CHAPTER NINE

FRANCESCO had been closeted with the hired wedding organiser since eight that morning—a cool, smooth blonde, with efficiency dripping from her beautifully manicured scarlet-tipped fingers.

Anna had done as she'd been asked and written her list of wedding guests, which she had handed over horribly conscious of the manic state of her hair—courtesy of Sholto's desire to explore every crinkly strand—and the baby dribble on the shoulder of her designer shirt.

Fancy labels didn't go with child-minding, and, regardless of what Francesco had to say on the matter, she was going to have to acquire a few bog-standard jeans and T-shirts.

The cool blonde had placed her list, together with the one faxed through from his cousin Silvana and, presumably, the one Francesco had supplied, into a slim leather briefcase and departed.

Musing on the unpalatable fact that she was being allowed very little input towards her own wedding, she gave a little leap of surprise when Sophia tucked her

hand beneath her elbow and crowed, 'The wedding organiser has gone. Now for the fun part!'

Turning startled eyes on the pretty brunette, Anna
visibly relaxed. 'I didn't see you coming—you made me
jump!'

Meeting Francesco's sister at dinner last night, she had
immediately taken to her. Lovely to look at, with sleek
dark hair flowing down to the middle of her narrow back,
dancing black eyes and a ready smile, she possessed a
warm, outgoing personality that had made Anna able to
endure ploughing through three of Peggy's excellent
courses beneath Francesco's brooding gaze, under the
explicit curve of his handsome mouth that reminded her
so forcibly of her soon-to-be sex slave status.

A shudder of awareness rippled down her spine at that
reminder, and Sophia soothed her. 'Every bride-to-be
gets the nervous attack. I was dreadful before my
wedding—I couldn't stay still for one small moment!
Here—' she tucked an oblong of smooth plastic into
Anna's hand '—Francesco said to give this to you. He
has opened an account—all you have to do is sign.'

'Where is he now?' The credit card was burning a
hole in he palm of her hand. She wanted to drop it! Her
throat tightened. She wanted to toss it on the ground in
front of his feet and loudly restate that she didn't want
his wretched money!

'He was going to look in on the baby, then shut
himself in his study to work, so forget him if you can. I
know you can't take your eyes off each other—probably
can't keep your hands off each other, either!' She
giggled. 'I have seen this—but this morning we are

going make the plastic work very hard, so hurry and get ready. We shop for your trousseau, silly!' she stated, when faced with Anna's blank stare. 'And Francesco tells me he is having a choice of wedding gowns flown over from Milan. We will have a hard time choosing—they will all be beautiful!'

Three hectic hours later Anna collapsed with thankfulness at a table outside a fashionable bistro, fanning her perspiring face and surreptitiously slipping her aching feet out of her shoes.

The sun was unseasonably hot, and Sophia had dragged her in and out of so many classy boutiques she'd lost count. At least she had acquired a couple of serviceable cotton skirts and cheap T-shirts—but the dreadfully expensive nightgown and matching negligee, not to mention a whole raft of wickedly sexy underwear that Sophia had proclaimed impossible to leave behind, threatened to give her terminal indigestion.

'There—this is good!' Sophia seated herself, the sea of carriers—some classy, one or two definitely down-market—flowing around her feet. 'We have an hour before Arnold arrives to collect us.' She picked up the menu. 'What shall we eat?'

In the end they chose herb omelettes with a simple green salad, and a glass of chablis. Sophia tipped her head on one side and said, 'I never thought the day would come when Francesco married. It is a joy to me to know I was wrong!' Her smile was mega-watt and full of warmth. 'He chose well—you will make him so happy!'

Anna gave her attention to the omelette to hide her bleak expression. Happy? It wasn't in her gift to make him happy. Satisfying him in bed until he tired of her was as good as it could get.

Anything to get her mind off that miserable track, she laid down her fork and asked as lightly as she could, 'So why didn't you think he'd marry? After all, he's got to be every girl's dream.' Breathtakingly handsome, fabulously wealthy, able to charm the birds out of the trees when the mood took him—what woman wouldn't go weak at the knees in his vicinity?

'Yes, and that's the problem.'

Sophia's serious response drew Anna's brows together in a puzzled frown. As far as she could tell there would be no problem as far as Francesco was concerned. Arm candy came with his status.

'It is not something we talk about.' Sophia sighed. 'But you are family now, and you have given him the blessing of a child.' She drained her wine glass. 'My brother never talks of it—he refuses to speak of it—but there should be no secrets in a family.'

Her dark eyes misted, and Anna saw that if Francesco refused to talk about whatever it was, then his sister was also finding it difficult.

'You see, a bad thing happened when we were children,' Sophia continued quietly. 'It saddens me to say this, but our mother had no heart, no love in her. She was a great beauty, a society darling, and to our father she was a great passion—an obsession, I suppose you could call it. When she left us he was a broken man. He changed overnight from being a normal sort of father to being cold and distant—he seemed to hate having his children around him.'

'She left you?' Anna couldn't make sense of that. 'She had two beautiful children who both needed her and a husband who adored her. Why leave? Did she fall in love with someone else?' How terrible!

'No. Now I am older I have put the picture together—with the help of people who knew the family at that time. I was barely four years old when she left, and I don't really remember her. But Francesco was ten, and her leaving hit him hard. He adored her. And of course Papa was a changed man. He took to drinking too much and not wanting his children around. Francesco had to be like both parents rolled into one. He looked after me.'

She fiddled with the stem of her glass and turned to ask a passing waiter for a refill. 'What happened was that Papa's business had hit a rough patch. He could no longer give our mother the magnificent lifestyle she demanded. She went away with someone who could. Falling in love had nothing to do with it. Francesco and I discovered that from the note she left Papa when we were going through his things after he died.'

She spread expressive hands. 'Francesco was twenty at that time, and already had females swarming all over him like bees at a honeypot. You wouldn't believe some of the lengths they went to—one had herself delivered in a big pretend cake, another got into his bed quite naked for him to find! But he ignored them all. He chose the occasional mistress with care, making sure they knew he wasn't asking for or giving any commitment,

and spent all his energies on getting the family busi-
nesses more profitable than they'd ever been.'

'So he saw all women as clones of your mother?
Only interested in his wealth?' Anna intuited, her heart
aching for the ten-year-old Francesco, whose beautiful,
adored mother had deserted him and his little sister with
no more thought than as to where her next suite of
diamonds would come from. No wonder he found it impossible to believe he could be loved for himself.

'*Precisamente!* He saw what loving such a self-
seeking woman had done to his father, decided it would
never happen to him, and became unable to trust any of
the female sex. A great big cynic!' She smiled widely.
'But no more!' She put her hand over Anna's as it lay
on the table, patted it. 'You have taught him how to trust
and how to love! And you can't know how grateful I am
to you for that—he so deserves to love and be loved!'

Unable to sleep, despite the two large glasses of wine
with dinner, which she and Sophia had companionably
lingered over, Anna stared into the darkness.

It should have been a relaxing evening. She and
Sophia had had fun bathing Sholto, and Sophia had
chattered non-stop throughout dinner. Francesco hadn't
put in an appearance—Peggy delivering a message that
he'd been called in to head office and would be delayed
until late.

It should have been relaxing. But it hadn't been.
Shocking herself, she'd found she'd really missed him,
and when Sophia had opined, 'When you are married
and living in his beautiful *palazzo* in Toscana it will be

different. My brother will not want to work so hard, be away from you and the gorgeous *bambino* for the smallest moment!' Anna had had to bite her tongue to stop herself blurting that it wouldn't be like that.

Somehow she had to maintain the façade that her marriage to Francesco would be the love-match that so obviously delighted his sister.

But pretending was hard.

When at half past ten Sophia had yawned and confessed that the excitement of trousseau-shopping had tired her out, and she couldn't wait for the morning when the wedding dresses would be arriving from Milan, Anna had gone to bed, too, not wanting to hang around waiting for a glimpse of Francesco because that would make her look needy.

She'd heard him return just after midnight. Acutely attuned to every move he made, she'd listened to his quiet footsteps, first visiting the nursery and then going to his room at the far end of the corridor.

Now, her eyes aching with the strain of staring into the darkness, she knew she had to go to him. What Sophia had told her had made a deep impression. It had explained much. Starting with his entrenched view that she, like the rest of the female sex, wanted only to get her hands on his wealth, to enjoy the kind of lifestyle that could be provided by a man with millions behind him.

Apparently he'd been targeted by gold-diggers since he'd hit his late teens—including the one who'd had herself delivered in a cake, and the other planting herself in his bed. The trauma of his mother's desertion, and the reason for it, etched on his heart, he'd become wary, distrustful of all females under ninety!

Hadn't he accused her of draping herself 'alluringly' on his private beach, hoping he'd happen along? Echoes of other distasteful attempts to snare him?

And hadn't he also said, quite unequivocally, that they had to put the past behind them and be civilized? Enter marriage for the sake of their child, with great sex the only thing going for them?

She slipped out of bed, snatching up the summerweight coverlet and draping it around her because her nightie, courtesy of Madame Laroche's excellent taste, was too revealing for a woman who was set on putting the record straight, not on seduction.

Put the past behind them, indeed! They could try, but it wouldn't go there!

His misconceptions about her were one huge stumbling block, and she was going to get rid of it!

Pushing his bedroom door open before her courage deserted her, she heard the shower in the *en suite* bathroom. Firmly she told herself she was not going to bottle out, turn tail and scurry back in wimpish haste to her own room. This had to be done if their future relationship was to have any meaning at all.

So, OK, he had seduced her, used her, dumped her— and had only offered marriage because she had given him the child he openly adored. He certainly didn't love her—never would. She would have to live with that. What she wouldn't live with was his jaundiced impression that she was nothing but a greedy schemer.

The shower stopped. Every last muscle in Anna's

body tensed to screaming point, and her bare toes dug into the pile of the plain fawn carpet. Unlike the room she occupied, this was severely masculine—that was her edgy thought just as a severely masculine male appeared in the doorway.

Stark naked.

In a ridiculous reflex action Anna snatched at the edges of the coverlet and enclosed her suddenly quivering body even more tightly. He was shatteringly beautiful. A magnificent torso, smooth and tanned, a stomach taut and flat as a board, a silky line of dark hair running down to cradle his manhood, long lower limbs in perfect proportion to his height.

She should look away.

She couldn't.

Her throat was too thick to get out the words that would explain her presence here in his room late at night, and they fled her brain completely when he strode towards her, his handsome mouth sardonically amused as he placed firm hands on her narrow shoulders and delivered, 'We must start on equal terms, *cara*.' And he removed the light coverlet from her oddly unresisting hands.

Hot colour flushed her face. She felt horribly exposed in the thin oyster-hued silk that skimmed her body to display barely concealed bountiful curves that sent dark colour flaring over his hard cheekbones and turned his eyes to smoke.

'What—what are you doing?' Anna gasped as he slid the thin ribbon straps down over her shoulders, not stopping until the creamy, rose-tipped mounds of her peaking breasts were exposed.

'What do you think?' Eyes shimmeringly intent, Francesco snatched a ragged breath. 'I am obliging my eager bride-to-be by taking what she is so enticingly offering.'

'But—' The vehement denial she'd been about to make was forgotten in a white-hot wash of addictive need as she felt the nightdress slip down over her hips and he took her mouth with ravishing hunger, plundering the sweet interior.

All control was lost.

Just as it had been that very first time. That was her helpless thought as honesty belatedly compelled her to admit that maybe this was what she had really come for. Maybe she had cloaked her need with the cover of setting him straight about her ignorance of his high financial status. That surely could have been more sensibly embarked upon in the cool, sober light of morning.

Her knees shaking beneath her, she deepened her response to his plundering mouth and lifted her arms, her fingers digging into his thick, still-damp hair. She was hot as a furnace all over, wanting to tell him she had never stopped loving him but not daring because he wouldn't believe her, gasping convulsively as she felt the burning strength of his arousal against her quivering tummy. She heard him give a raw growl low in his throat as he broke the kiss and swept her up in his arms, to come down beside her on the massive bed.

He spread the bright shimmer of her hair against the dark cover, his lips on her forehead, on the tip of her small nose, his eyelids lowered over gleaming, sensual silver.

'When I look at you, I want you. I hunger,' he

murmured roughly. He lowered his head to take a pouting nipple between his lips, expert hands shaping her body.

The sensation made her squirm beneath him, whimpering as his mouth roved from one sensitively peaking tip to the other, until she was driven to plead, with aching desperation, 'Make love to me, Francesco!'

CHAPTER TEN

IN A tangle of limbs and rumpled sheets Francesco slept, while Anna, her cheek against the warm satin of his impressive chest, listened to the steady beat of his heart, breathed in the intoxicating male scent of him and tried to hold onto the magic.

The magic of pretending they were back where they once had been, in those lost enchanted days beneath the hot Italian sun, when she'd been so ecstatically happy, believing he meant it when he vowed he loved her as much as she loved him.

She'd known he was a fantastic lover—had first-hand unforgettable experience—but tonight had been something else. Something driven. He had dominated her, thoroughly possessed her, and the ecstasy he had given her had been so intense she'd thought she might die of it.

Sex slave.

Reality hit hard. Made her eyes well with tears, her throat tighten. She'd once told herself she hated him. But she didn't. For her sins, she couldn't stop loving him, but that didn't mean she had to leap into bed with him with shamefully eager wantonness. Especially as she knew darn well that he didn't love her, actually despised her for what he thought she was.

'What is wrong, *amante*?'

So he hadn't been asleep! His voice shook her rigid—purring with contentment, his accent more pronounced than usual, reeking with the dominant male satisfaction of knowing his sex slave was his for the merest crook of his little finger!

'Your beautiful body has gone quite tense,' he drawled, with a lacing of amusement. He rolled over onto his side, his long, muscular, shatteringly sexy body partly covering her. 'I shall relax you,' he stated, with indolently sensual intent, a long-fingered hand sliding over her tummy, where the muscles tensed, down to the apex of her thighs.

Something fierce and hot shot through her responsive body, melting her bones. He could always make that happen. And she was always helpless, the fire in her greedily leaping to reach the fire in him.

'No!' Desperate to save herself from once more shaming herself by demonstrating what a complete and utter pushover she was—his for the taking whenever he wanted her—Anna shot up against the heaped pillows. 'You just don't get it, do you?'

'Get what?' Vibrant amusement still glimmered in his hooded eyes. He was still looming over her. She flattened her palms against the solid wall of his chest, pushed with all her might—and didn't budge him an inch.

Emotionally all over the place, she blurted, not caring how much of herself she was revealing, 'I love you!'

Stinging silence met her self-betrayal. Then, eyes

suddenly hostile, Francesco pulled away from her, clipping, 'There's no need to say that. What we just shared was great sex. Don't spoil it by lying.'

Infuriated, she slid off the bed in haste, to put distance between them, her heartfelt but probably misguided confession embarrassing her. 'Lying's your territory, not mine!' she charged heatedly, humiliation washing over her—because she'd bared her soul to him and he'd unforgivably accused her of lying, of putting a pretty gloss on their troubled relationship. A gloss he found distasteful because he judged it to be insincere.

'Meaning?' His voice was black ice.

'Pretending to be a practically penniless peasant, not coming clean about who you were.' She confronted him, snatching the coverlet from the floor, where he'd dropped it, and wrapping it with savagery around her nakedness. Voice spiked with bitterness, she put in with derision, 'The cheap and nasty chain you wore was a nice touch! A very convincing stage prop! Does deceit come naturally to you, or did you have lessons? Don't you dare accuse *me* of lying!'

Heading for the door as fast as her feet would carry her, she paused, dragged in a giant breath and imparted, 'I came here to make you understand that I'm *not* one of the gold-diggers you're so wary of. I had no idea you could pay off the national debt and still have change!' she exaggerated wildly, and gave a 'so there!' flounce as she turned again for the door.

She was stopped in her tracks when he launched at her, 'You knew. You'd seen photographs of me in the press. You admitted it, if you remember. And if your father was expecting to entertain your new "penniless peasant" of a lover, why did he ask me for a million sterling five minutes after I crossed the threshold? Your big mistake was in not advising him to wait patiently for the plums to fall into his lap.'

Absolutely stunned, Anna could only stare as he leant over and switched off the bedside light, plunging the room into darkness. Sounding ice-cool, he advised, 'Face up to what you are. I have. After all,' he added, dry as dust, 'you've got what you set out to get. Cut the histrionics and we might make a reasonable attempt at a future life together. Go to bed.'

Anna headed for the nursery next morning feeling as if she were sleepwalking. Her head was pounding and her puffy eyes bore witness to a prolonged crying jag.

She'd spent the rest of the night after Francesco had so calmly dismissed her wondering if it could possibly be true. Had Dad really brazenly asked him for a million pounds? The very idea made her stomach roll over.

Remembering his crazy idea of starting a safari park, in yet another ridiculous scheme to recoup the money he'd lost, she had sickly acknowledged that it could be so.

She had no idea how he'd known the Italian owned much more than the shirt on his back. *She* certainly hadn't. But, he had as good as accused her of putting her father up to asking for such a massive amount, and no amount of denials on her part would make him believe her.

Her last hope of gaining his respect, if not his love, had vanished. And she didn't know how she could spend the rest of her life with him, loving him, needing him, knowing he thought so badly of her.

He was right about one thing. The sex was out of this world. And at the moment everything in that department was fine for him. But he didn't love her, never would, and the time would inevitably come when he looked for new challenges. And then she would have nothing of him. They would be just two strangers with nothing to bind them but their child. And when their child was grown, setting out on his own, she would have nothing. She really didn't think she could face such a future.

Yet how could she deprive darling Sholto of two parents who loved him to bits. Not to mention all the massive advantages of being the son of Francesco Mastroianni? How could she refuse to go through with the marriage and then live with the dreadful and pressing fear that her baby's father would do all within his limitless power to claim him?

Not forgetting her parents. Despite Mum being too feeble to put her foot down, to take control of the family finances before things had got so way out of hand, and despite Dad being so ebulliently sure that he knew better than a coachload of financial advisors, she loved them both. Refuse to marry Francesco and the years that were left to them would be lived in grinding poverty.

Her headache was getting worse by the second. Determined to stop going over and over her dreadful situation, at least for as long as it took to bath and feed little Sholto, she put a pallid smile on her face and opened the door.

'For once I beat you to it.' Francesco's lithe lean body

dwarfed the nursing chair. Sholto, wearing a fresh white sleeper suit, was cradled in his arms, blissfully asleep. 'I changed and fed him,' he claimed proudly. 'It is not so difficult.'

'So I see,' Anna mumbled, through lips that felt as stiff as cement. Last night might not have happened, she registered. Things had been said by both of them, accusations hurled like bricks. And now they had to be forgotten. He was being civilised!

Sex was the only level on which she could fleetingly reach him. She couldn't touch him on any emotional level. He had put his distaste for what he thought she was to one side for the sake of Sholto's future well-being. All his emotions were centred on his tiny son, as he now demonstrated as he ran the back of a forefinger softly over the baby's downy cheek and imparted, 'After the marriage we will spend most of our time at my home in Tuscany, where he will have all the freedom and space to run and play in air that is not polluted. I will teach him to fish and ride, and he will grow tall and strong.'

Easing himself from the low chair, he laid the contented baby back in his cot, straightened and announced, 'We will have a nanny.'

Just like that! Rebellion sparked inside her, but she was careful to keep her voice low and level as she asked, 'Don't I have a say in that? I don't need a nanny to look after him.'

Already she was feeling dreadfully deprived of the only time she now found anything approaching real happiness. That precious early-morning hour spent bathing, dressing, playing with and feeding her baby.

How intolerable it would be to have a hired nanny—
no matter how good her references, how kind she
was—taking over!

Was he intending to completely sideline her? Turn her
into a cipher, a creature of no importance, only useful
in his bed—until he tired of her?

'Perhaps not,' he conceded. 'But consider—when
you are pregnant again you will be grateful for just a
little help. Especially when you have a newborn and an
energetic toddler to entertain. And maybe another on the
way in the blink of an eye?'

'I can't believe you actually said that,' Anna told him
in a strangled tone. Shut away in the back of beyond,
unable to speak the language, with no friends or family
to support her, producing one baby after another—like
on a conveyor belt! The mental image alone was enough
to give her hysterics! 'You want loads more children?'

His narrowed-eyes appraisal was full of amusement
as he said, 'Given our track record, *amante*, it's a
foregone conclusion. Swept away by lust just about
covers it, wouldn't you say?'

An unsubtle reminder of her wanton behaviour last
night, when the thought of precautions had not entered
her head. Or his. On purpose? Did he intend to keep
her permanently pregnant, surrounded by so many
children she wouldn't have the time or energy to notice
when he strayed?

Her ashen face did the impossible and turned even
whiter. As if properly seeing her for the first time, he
gave an impatient click of his tongue, swept his hand
beneath her elbow and escorted her to the door. 'You

look terrible. Go back to bed and rest for a couple of hours. Peggy will bring breakfast to you at ten.'

Opening the door to her room, he placed a hand in the small of her back, eased her over the threshold and drawled, 'And, by the way, if wearing those ugly things is your idea of shaming me, of paying me back for seeing through your attempt to bamboozle me last night, you've failed.'

He meant the baggy T-shirt and undeniably cheap and badly cut jeans she'd bought from the market around which she'd dragged a disapproving and reluctant Sophia on that shopping trip.

Rallying as he began to close her into her bedroom, furious that he should automatically assume that her emotionally riven declaration of love was a pack of lies, she rounded on him, faint colour brushing her pale cheeks.

'You are the most self-centred male I have ever met! Everything I do or say has to be meant for you, doesn't it? Well, listen up—every thought I have *doesn't* revolve round you. I bought this cheap gear to wear to save that fancy stuff you've lumbered me with!' She was getting into her stride, almost enjoying herself—and the startled light in those smoke-grey eyes. 'Sholto loves his morning bath, which means he squirms and wriggles and soaks me. And he dribbles when I burp him. So, no, you didn't even enter my head when I dressed this morning!'

And she closed the door on his astonishment.

CHAPTER ELEVEN

FRANCESCO tossed his suit jacket over the fax machine, loosened his tie. The room he used as his home office was his only oasis of peace.

Returning after an absence of more than two weeks, he had found the large London house uncomfortably full of relatives. Anna's parents had been fussing over the wedding gifts that had, apparently, been arriving by the truck-load. Declining to join them in the general oohs and aahs, he had been almost knocked off his feet by his niece's exuberant greetings, and had only been able to extricate himself from her stranglehold around his neck with the arrival of Fabio, his brother-in-law.

'Cristina—let Zio Francesco breathe!' He had grabbed the squirming six-year-old by the waist and unplastered her from her uncle's chest. 'He will admire your bridesmaid's dress later, at a time of his convenience! Right now he has things to do.'

After exchanging a wry grin with the older man, he had found the wedding organiser holding court with her usual brisk efficiency in the ground-floor sitting room with Sophia, as he would have expected, nodding, agreeing and exclaiming excitedly. Anna had been sitting mute, with a face like stone.

The wedding was two days away. He wanted it over. Although he'd been back for a scant twenty minutes he was already finding the preliminaries irritating, making him edgy. He had never thought the day would dawn when he'd actually embrace the notion of marriage to a proven gold-digger without running the proverbial mile, when he'd be positively aching to be alone with his family. His wife. His baby son.

But it had. And that state of affairs surely meant his mental faculties had been severely impaired! Or was he a sensible guy, sure of his ability to handle the future, doing what was right for all concerned?

His hard, sensual mouth twisted wryly. What was that old saying? Never make a wish, it might come true.

Once entranced, besotted, eager as a callow youth—his dearest wish had been to make Anna his wife. Now that wish was about to come true. But how different from the wedded bliss he had envisaged!

And Anna? Her wish to marry into great wealth was about to be granted. But she acted as if she were about to keep an appointment to have her limbs severed from her torso without benefit of anaesthetic rather than go through the ceremony that would see the fulfilment of her avaricious dreams.

Had she, too, painted a rosy mind-picture of their glittering future together? Spoiled and pampered, with an adoring, blinkered husband dancing attendance on her slightest whim?

If so, tough! He wasn't his father!

Impatiently, Francesco ran a finger round the inside of his shirt collar and undid the top button. Something had to be sorted out. Now. They couldn't spend the rest of their lives together indulging in not so lightly veiled warfare.

The past two weeks or so had been spent visiting his company head offices across the world. Promoting, demoting, putting the most able and trustworthy managers in place to take the burden of day-to-day decisions off his shoulders in order to leave him free to spend much more time with his son. Little Sholto would grow to manhood knowing that his father loved him, wanted to be around him, spent quality time with him, would be there for him whatever happened.

Now all that had to be done was to reach an understanding with his bride-to-be.

He found her in the garden. Sholto lay on a rug in the dappled shade. His rounded limbs were bare, punching joyfully energetic holes in the warm late-afternoon air, and Anna was beside him, propped up on one elbow, gently tickling his tummy, her lovely face softened and glowing, her abundant hair precariously massed on the top of her head.

For long moments he stayed where he was, his heart so full he thought it might burst. Love for his tiny son, he rationalized. Nothing else. This overwhelming emotion could be nothing else.

He had loved Anna once—loved her beyond reason. But that had died at the exact and damning moment when her father had tried to part him from a hefty wad of the folding stuff. He still lusted after her. He only had to look at her and his whole body went into overdrive, aching to possess her. Lust wasn't pretty, but it was reality. And he always faced reality.

His impressive shoulders squared, he strolled forward. 'In two weeks he has grown,' he observed, annoyed by the definitely husky quality of his voice. His annoyance intensified by a thousand per cent when he noted how she stiffened at his arrival on the idyllic scene.

Stifling the desire to make the cynical observation that she didn't go as rigid as a plank of toughened steel when he touched her, but melted into his arms like warm honey, he lifted his son and held him aloft in his arms, grinning like the besotted fool he was, exulting as his action produced crowing sounds in the precious infant.

'He smiled at me!' he enthused, forgetting his future bride's less than welcoming body language for the moment, revelling in the bubbly, crinkly movement of the tiny mouth. 'I swear it wasn't just wind!'

In this mood her son's father was irresistible, Anna thought sourly. But no way was she about to succumb, give way, let her heart reach out to him with love and then wait for the inevitable cruel accusation or unpleasant revelation to hit her. She would not live her life seesawing from one violent emotion to another.

She stood, brushing non-existent creases from the fine cotton skirt she was wearing with a matching jade green sleeveless top, and Francesco said, with a touch of dryness that made her ears sting, 'Don't let me drive you away! It is good for our son to have the company of both parents.'

'Don't flatter yourself! It's time for his evening bath and feed,' Anna countered matter-of-factly, refusing to let him get to her on any level. No way would she allow him to think his presence had her scuttling away like a frightened rabbit. She wouldn't give him the ego-trip of thinking he could affect her behaviour. 'You can carry him up to the nursery and hang around if you want to,' she conceded calmly, and set off towards the house.

Even though her heart was pattering like mad, she was proud of the way she'd managed to let him know she could take his presence or leave it. She nearly fell over her feet when he, following with Sholto, confirmed warmly, 'I would like that. And tonight we dine out. It is arranged. Sophia will take the monitor—she is looking forward to babysitting. You and I need to talk away from the eyes and ears of our assembled family members.'

Taking her seat at the pricily secluded and intimate table in one of London's most fashionable restaurants, Anna felt, ridiculously, like a fluttery girl embarking on her first date.

Her escort, eye-swivellingly handsome in his white dinner jacket, had turned all female heads as they'd been shown to their table, and Anna couldn't blame them. Francesco Mastroianni was one class act. She was probably the envy of every female in the place. But she wasn't going to let that go to her head, because she knew that nothing was what it seemed. Very far from it.

And she wasn't going to get flustered because those silvery grey eyes of his were quite definitely appreciative and amazingly proprietorial, nor react when he remarked softly, his accent pronounced, 'You are very beautiful. The dress suits you. But, like me, every man in the room is probably wanting to remove it from you.'

She would not blush. She would *not*! Neither would she give way to the silly impulse to pluck at the dipping neckline of the understatedly sexy red dress and simper, Oh, this old rag!

Instead, she laid aside the menu she'd been given and said, 'This is your idea. You order for me. You said you wanted to talk. Well, I've got something I want to say to you.'

'And that is?' One sable brow arched lazily, his gorgeous mouth taking on the slow half-smile that infuriated her because it usually meant he was patronising her.

So she said, 'My parents tell me they are to live at your London address. Permanently. Everything thrown in—even a part-time job of sorts at your London office for Dad.'

'And they are not pleased?'

'You know damn well they are!' It was a dreadful struggle to keep her voice down, to button her lip as Francesco gave their order, indicated that the wine waiter should open the bottle of champagne that had been waiting on ice for their arrival.

Since their arrival two days ago her parents had hardly stopping singing the praises of their so-generous future son-in-law—going on and on about how much they were looking forward to living here, being able to go to the theatre whenever they wanted to, wander round the shops and galleries when the mood took them, take in all the sights, and wasn't it a blessing that they both got on so well with Peggy and Arnold, who were to be kept on to look after them? It had been the first she had heard of it, and it rankled.

'So? Your point is?'

'That you arranged all that without telling me. You really know how to make sure I know just how unimportant I am.' Her sense of exclusion had been shockingly painful. Her eyes sparked emerald fire, wild rose colour flooding her cheeks as she accused, 'And my wedding—*you* briefed the blonde iceberg. I wasn't consulted about anything!'

'But she kept you up to speed?' He was fingering the stem of his glass, and though she was doubting her own eyes, was he really looking just slightly discomfited?

'I was *told* what flowers I would have, what food and wine would be served at the reception and so on, if that's what you mean. All done and dusted—with the distinct impression that if I wanted the slightest change I'd be told to go and sit in a corner, and not speak until spoken to!'

Not that she cared what arrangements were made, because as far as she was concerned the ceremony would be the equivalent of being handed a life sentence, bound to a man who viewed her as a necessary evil.

Francesco leaned forward, his laid-back façade showing signs of cracking, 'If there is something you're not happy with then it's not too late to change it,' he assured her rapidly, taking the wind out of her sails. 'She is, I am told, the best wedding organiser around, but—'

'No,' Anna put in with deflated honesty. 'There's nothing I or anyone could object to.' So he was willing to take her concerns on board? It was news to her! 'It was the principle of the thing.'

'Of course. I'm—' He broke off impatiently as the deferential waiter served their first course, and as soon as they were alone again resumed. 'I'm sorry you haven't been consulted. My fault. Truth is, the last few weeks have been hectic. There were decisions to be made. I made them, acted on them. That's how I operate. But—' he smiled at her, making her defenceless heart flip '—I shall teach myself to think twice where you have concerns. You won't be kept in the dark in future. Starting now.'

His eyes held hers, reaching her, and for a moment she felt as if she were floating out of her body. She despised herself for still craving this man she loved to bits, even though she knew he saw her as a greedy liar, but her flesh trembled in reaction to the rough velvet of his voice as he told her, 'As you know, your father's debts have been cleared, and I now own Rylands. They were happy to sell to me. Apparently your mother has long wanted to move to somewhere more easily managed. And it seemed like a good idea to offer them the permanent use of my London home. Besides,' he intoned flatly, as if what he had to say was distasteful to him, 'I thought a token position on the board might stop your father from filling my garden with wild animals.'

Mutely, Anna nodded, resolutely ignoring the jibe about wild animals because it made her feel ill, concentrating on her mother's astounding confession.

When her parents had broken the news that they'd be living permanently at Francesco's London address she'd asked Mum if she would miss her family home, and she'd confessed no, not at all. She'd suggested selling up and cutting their losses to Dad many times, but he'd always flatly refused to entertain the idea. It was her family home and he wasn't going to see her lose it because of a few business setbacks. He would never forgive himself. In the end she had had to put her foot down—they'd almost quarrelled—and then their saviour, in the form of the generous Francesco, had happened along.

His smile was back as he explained, 'Major renovation work is soon to start on the house and grounds. And, if you agree, I'd like it to be kept in the family. In the normal course of events the house would have been part of our son's heritage. As you know, we will spend most of our time in Tuscany, but Sholto needs to learn something of his English roots. Rylands would be ideal for summer holidays—a traditional British Christmas, maybe. What do you think?'

He was actually asking her opinion instead of letting her know through a third party after the decision had been made! The fact that his prime concern was what was right for his son was something she would have to learn to live with. Her needs and wants didn't come into it. The knowledge was chilling.

'You're right.' He always was—or thought he was! But in this instance she agreed with him. 'Having a base in the English countryside will be good for Sholto.' And all the dozens of other children he expected her to give him!

She laid down her fork, her appetite disappearing like dew in hot summer sun, as Francesco said, 'I wanted to talk to you, discuss our future.' His beautiful mouth twisted wryly, 'To date we have been like duellists, circling each other, waiting for the opening to strike—apart from that one unforgettable night when you came to my bed, and that ended sourly, too. It mustn't go on,' he stated, with a sincerity that sent shivers up her spine. 'We are to be married. We have a son. The only sensible thing to do is to forget everything that has gone before, and go forward together in harmony.'

He raised his champagne flute and gave her the smile that always managed to splinter her heart. 'A toast to our future. Let it be calm. No more fighting! I give you peace in our time!' His eyes were wicked, sexy, warm, reminding her forcibly of the time on the island when happiness for her had been his glance, his smile, his touch, drenching her in the sadness of loss.

Make the best of a bad job, she translated with an inner shudder. Hardly the best recipe for wedded bliss. But then she hadn't expected that, had she?

She stared at the glass, at the straw-coloured liquid alive with diamond-bright bubbles, and her throat closed up. With inner reluctance she slowly raised her glass to his. No more fighting. Sweep the past—the hurt—under the carpet. Take whatever the future held with calm stoicism. Never complain, never look into the past, never be seen without a serene smile on her face.

A marriage like tramlines. Running parallel, never meeting except on the most basic physical level. Wham-bam, thank you, ma'am! Always being careful. Careful not to say or imply anything that might bring up things that had been said or done, nasty accusations that had to stay hidden under that carpet.

She didn't know if she was going to be able to live like

that. She owed it to herself to try—again—to make him believe her. Remembering how he had met her earlier attempts with cringe-making cynicism, she shivered.

After recklessly draining her glass, she watched him refill it as pork roulades and individual dishes of beautifully cooked vegetables were placed on the table. She didn't think she could eat any of it, and told him flatly, 'I might be about to break this peace you suddenly seem to find less taxing than sniping at each other, but—and this is important to me—you have to know that I had no idea of who you were or what you were worth until weeks after you dumped me.'

She bit her lip. His eyes were cold, his mouth tight. He was determined not to believe her! But she'd started this, so she would finish it.

Her voice firm, belying the quaking going on inside her, she said, 'Cissie showed me an old magazine. There was an article about you—your successes in the financial field.' Pointless to mention the simpering arm candy. 'Know this about me—I am *not* the same as your mother.'

Silence. Just the muted chatter of the other diners.

'Sophia has been talking,' he said, with nerve-shredding quietness. Dull colour laid a path over his angular cheekbones and his mouth was tight with displeasure.

But all Anna could see was a bewildered ten-year-old boy whose adored mother had suddenly disappeared from his life. And whose father, just when he needed him most, had turned his back on him and the tiny sister he found himself responsible for. He would have played with Sophia, who'd been little more than a baby, given her the love she wasn't getting from any other quarter, tried to take the place of both parents, growing up with responsibility, a strong sense of duty deeply ingrained.

Hence his decision to marry the mother of his own son—despite her being, in his eyes, just another greedy woman on the make. No matter what she said in her own defence, circumstances had conspired to make any belief in her impossible. But she could, and would, defend his sister.

Leaning forward, her eyes brimming with compassion, she told him softly, 'Don't be cross with Sophia. She's so pleased about the wedding—she just came out with it, said she'd never thought she'd live to see the day. I asked why, naturally, and she told me about your mother only marrying your father for the money that could buy her the glittering lifestyle she wanted. Then leaving him for some other well-heeled guy when she saw the supply was in danger of drying up. How your father was so devastated he didn't even want to have anything to do with his children. She said I was family now, and should know.'

Lifting her slender shoulders in a tiny shrug, she added, 'You're her big brother and she loves you, and she's happy for you, thinking you've finally found a woman you can trust enough to love.' Her voice flattened. 'I didn't prick her bubble—tell her how very wrong she is because you don't trust me at all. And you certainly don't love me.'

But he had done. Once. She was sure of it now. Her heart was hurting, her throat tightening as knowledge of what she'd lost swamped her.

She'd thought of little else since he'd exploded that

bombshell about what had happened the night he'd dumped her, washed his hands of her and walked away. It added up. It was the missing piece of the jigsaw.

He had loved her. When they'd met on Ischia he'd concealed his true identity because he'd wanted to be loved for himself, not his wealth. He had meant every word when he'd said he loved her.

But Dad, with his usual bull-at-a-gate tactics, had killed that love dead as the dodo. He must have recognised his daughter's new boyfriend from the pages of the financial papers he took, and had barged straight in and asked for massive investment in that crazy safari park idea, convinced that everyone would see his latest surefire money-making scheme as the world-beater he alone thought it was.

She was sure it had happened that way, and Francesco's earlier reference to wild animals in his garden clinched it. Didn't it just!

She toyed with her cutlery, not able to eat. And, no, she hadn't broached the subject with her father, insisted he tell her exactly what he'd said to Francesco that evening. Because if he'd confirmed what she already believed she would have blown her top, accused him of ruining her chance of true happiness, causing so much ill-feeling that her approaching wedding day would be even more of an uncomfortable farce than it was going to be.

Besides, she loved her eccentric father unconditionally. Creating a real rift between them would be dreadful. What was done was done, the outcome unchangeable. Because of what had happened to him when he was a bewildered, vulnerable small boy Francesco was programmed to suspect any woman who vowed she loved him of having ulterior and mercenary motives.

'I'm sorry. This isn't working.' A slight gesture had the waiter gliding forward with the bill, and Anna watched his eyes frost over, his strong, lean face hard as the transaction was completed.

He stood, every line of his magnificent body tense, his eyes inward-looking, and Anna scrambled to her feet, her legs shaking like an ill-set jelly.

Their cosy date, with him spelling out the slick, totally unreal guidelines for their future, had been blown out of the water because she'd opened her big mouth, told him things he didn't want to hear.

He would never believe she hadn't had a clue as to who he really was when their baby was conceived, and he despised her for trying to tell him otherwise. He was furious because Sophia had spilled the beans about what their mother had done, how their father had behaved towards them as children. It was a period of his life he never talked about, and he obviously resented her knowing.

Had he, like her, come to the conclusion that their marriage was on the rocks before it even happened?

A black cab was already waiting. Francesco handed her in. He had a whole lot of thinking to do. Finding the truth was now imperative—and that included a long overdue talk with her father.

He'd been off his head to have believed he could put a shiny gloss on their future—paste over the fissure-like cracks, pretend they didn't exist.

Insisting on marriage hadn't all been about his son. Anna herself was at the core of it. At last he was honest enough to admit that he still loved her. He wanted to believe she still loved him. But if what came out of his conversation with her father failed to convince, then he was not going to follow in his own father's footsteps and enter a marriage where one partner loved and the other just took.

Initially he'd believed he could make the marriage work for the sake of his son. Rub along, shut out the past, be civilised—with the bonus, of course, of great sex. But now that he'd finally faced up to the fact that no woman had ever been able to affect him as she did, that he loved her, he knew it could never work. It would fail, as his parents' marriage had, leaving him bitter and hurting.

'I'll walk.' He gave the address, passed notes to the driver, turned back to her, his eyes bleak. 'I'll see you at the altar.'

Maybe.

CHAPTER TWELVE

'You look so beautiful!' Beatrice Maybury's eyes were misty as Sophia, elegant in a suit of amber-coloured silk, finished fastening the myriad of tiny buttons at the back of the elaborately beaded white satin wedding gown and adjusted the filmy veil.

'Fantastica!' Sophia sighed. 'So romantic—Francesco is a lucky man!'

Anna tried to smile.

Difficult.

There was nothing remotely romantic about this wedding.

Sophia fussing, Cristina preening, proud as a peacock in her lemon-coloured wild silk bridesmaid's dress, hopping from one foot to the other in excitement, demanding, 'Is it nearly time to go yet?' Mum sitting in regal splendour in her blue and gold brocade coat and amazing hat, nursing Sholto and looking dotingly at everything she laid her eyes on, the coming ceremony itself—all this was nothing but an elaborate stage set, with herself as one of the principal actors, playing her part in a fantasy of cruel unreality.

She hadn't seen Francesco since they'd left the restaurant.

'It's bad luck for the groom to see his bride so close to the wedding,' Mum had informed her. 'He's booked into a hotel—you'll see him at the altar!' Too interested in trying to decide which shoes went best with her mother-of-the-bride outfit, she had failed to notice the bleakness in her daughter's eyes.

The strangely chilling mood he'd been in when they'd parted had given her the impression that he'd washed his hands of her. Standing at the altar with her was the very last thing he wanted!

It was a horrible situation, she thought with utter misery, her self-esteem flat on the floor. He was only marrying her for the sake of the tiny son he so obviously adored, and she'd allowed herself to be as good as blackmailed into accepting him. Which would be OK, she supposed glumly, if she really *was* the sneaky money-grubber he believed she was.

But she wasn't! She'd stopped being blinkered and admitted she still loved the brute! And that made everything so very much worse!

She'd made one last desperate attempt to convince him of her integrity, but that had had the effect of changing him from someone who was willing to sweep the past under the carpet, to make the best of a bad job with a semblance of grace, in to someone who gave the impression that he never wanted to set eyes on her again!

'Stop daydreaming!' Sophia chided affectionately, putting a bouquet of white roses into her trembling hands. 'The cars are here.'

And so was her father. Looking good in his hired morning suit, a white carnation in his buttonhole, proud as punch as he took in his daughter's wedding finery.

As soon as they were alone he gave her a gentle hug, being careful not to squash pristine perfection, bringing tears to film her eyes. He was her father, and she loved him, and she knew he loved her, but he had been the cause of Francesco's unshakeable distrust of her.

'Nervous, poppet? Don't be—you'll make Bride Of The Year, and good old Dad's here to make safe passage!'

Too churned up inside to ask him what he was talking about, she found out, to her horror, when they walked through the outer door to face a small army of photographers, pushing, crowding, firing questions. Her head was swimming as Dad, with the help of the uniformed driver, allowed her to gain the sanctuary of the car without too much loss of dignity for the short drive.

There would be more of them waiting at the church she guessed. She supposed with a lurch of her already churning stomach that the marriage of one of the world's most eligible bachelors to a nobody made a story of sorts.

Cinderella!

Her heart wrenched. Without the happy ending!

'Poppet—I'm sorry. It's all my fault,' William Maybury said gruffly as the car purred forward.

'Don't be stupid,' Anna muttered tiredly. The photographers weren't snapping like crazy because of *him*. It was all down to who Francesco was.

'No—listen. I had a long chat with your young man last night. He asked me to go to his hotel. It was late when I got back, and you'd gone to bed, and this morning it's been hectic, so—'

'Dad, I don't want to talk. Not now. Please!' Her face pale and set, she turned her head away.

She simply could not bear to hear yet another paean of praise for the paragon! She couldn't blame her parents for being overwhelmed by the generosity that would enable them to live out their lives in luxury and security—they were practically unable to talk of anything else and she could understand that—but she didn't want to hear any more. Their future security had been bought at a mile-high price to herself!

Doing her best to ignore the photographers, Anna entered the fashionable church on her father's arm and saw Francesco waiting. Tall, achingly handsome, his morning suit clothing the perfection of his lithe body with elegance and style.

So her vague doubts that he'd show at all, that he'd washed his hands of her, had been unfounded. Her steps faltered. In a way it would have been better if he had left her standing at the altar! It would have been a clean break. She would have got over it. Eventually. Living the rest of her life loving him, knowing he thought she was—

'Chin up, poppet.' Her father's hand tightened on her elbow, urging her forward. 'Everything's absolutely fine, I promise!'

What the heck did he know? was her irreverent thought as his hand fell away and she found herself standing at Francesco's side.

He was looking at her, his too attractive features set, his eyes dark with emotion as they raked her pale face and huge haunted eyes. His voice was thick as he murmured, low and emotive, 'I love you Anna. *Love you.*'

The ceremony passed in a blur, Anna's head spinning, asking herself the same questions over and over. Had he really said that? Or had she misheard? A panic-induced, hopeless illusion? And, if he *had* said it, was it because he'd taken one look at her and, fearing she'd take flight, grab her little son and run, said the one thing guaranteed to root her to the spot?

It seemed no time at all before they were in the car to take them to the reception at some fancy hotel or other. The blonde iceberg had told her which one but she hadn't really taken it in.

'Did you mean what you said?' she questioned tightly, her tummy flipping.

He settled his long, elegant frame at her side and the car moved forward. His smouldering eyes moved over her. He took both her trembling hands in his. 'You are unbelievably beautiful. How could I not mean every word? I love you, *cara.*' He lifted her hands to his lips, turning them over to place softly lingering kisses in her palms, and her heart jerked painfully.

Was he just saying that? Using lavish helpings of that devastating charm he could conjure out of thin air just to keep her sweet until the public ordeal of the reception was over? His ego wouldn't stand the humiliation of having his new bride look one iota less than totally ecstatic.

Or did he mean it? How could he?

He raised his head, said something in his own language that sounded like a violent expletive. Then, 'We have arrived. There's no time to say what I must. An-na—' he cupped her face briefly '—trust me. I love you, and I swear I will prove it to you for the rest of my life!'

His avowal threw her off balance. He looked and sounded so sincere. And the way he held her hand and didn't let go until they were seated for the banquet, the focus of two hundred pairs of eyes, almost convinced her that a miracle had happened.

She so wanted to be convinced. And she allowed herself to be as the lavish wedding feast progressed and his eyes rarely left hers. They were the love-drenched eyes of the man she had first fallen in love with on that sun-soaked Italian island almost a year ago, and all doubts fled when, under cover of the applause and laughter at the end of Fabio's best man speech, Francesco reached into an inner pocket and slid a huge sparkling yellow diamond onto her finger above the plain gold band.

'I noticed you don't wear the ring I more or less forced on you—with such gross insensitivity.'

'You were impatient,' she excused, green eyes huge. 'I couldn't make up my mind. In any case.' Her small chin came up. 'I didn't want anything from you that wasn't given with love.'

Smouldering silver eyes met hers, and his voice was thick as he confided, briefly touching the ring that glittered on her finger, 'I chose this for you because the blonde stone reminded me of your lovely hair. It was in my pocket as I drove to Gloucestershire all those months ago. I was going to ask you to be my wife. It was chosen with love.'

He had loved her then, had wanted to marry her. Then everything had gone pear-shaped. Dad had blundered in and ruined everything. The stark reminder of cold reality sent an icy spasm round her heart and her eyes brimmed.

Nothing had changed. Not really. How could it when whenever she tried to convince him that she'd had no idea of who he was when they'd met he as good as accused her of lying? His private opinion of her must still be rock-bottom.

She couldn't fault his efforts to do just what he'd suggested in that restaurant—sweep what had happened under the carpet and put a glossy veneer of togetherness on their marriage. But—

'We have to talk. Properly talk,' she mumbled raggedly, hating the thought of living with a much-loved husband who, deep in the secret places of his heart, believed she was only with him for what she could get out of him. His protestations of love would only be made to ensure their marriage wasn't a battleground, an unfit arena for his son's upbringing.

'Of course.' He took her hand in his. 'Later.' His charismatic smile lit his spectacular features as he stood, drawing her with him. 'We are now expected to lead the dancing.'

Aware of music coming from the ballroom, and the gradual exodus of guests from the lavishly appointed dining room, Anna swallowed a sigh.

The show must go on!

Pinning a smile on her face, she allowed herself to be swept into a slow waltz, melting into the lean, hard strength of his body because she couldn't help herself, willing herself to believe that a miracle could happen, that he really had changed his mind about her, really did love her.

She snapped out of the dreamy state of complete capitulation that being held in his arms always induced when Fabio tapped him on his shoulder and claimed her.

Later, halfway through a dance with someone whose name she couldn't remember, had perhaps never known, she excused herself on the grounds that her feet were killing her, took a glass of champagne from a passing waiter, and went to find somewhere secluded to sit.

As arranged, Peggy and Arnold had taken Sholto home to be fed, changed and put down to sleep, and Francesco had done his duty, dancing with her mother, his sister and his cousin Silvana.

Finding a chair against a far wall, she sat, her eyes homing in on her husband, now dancing up close and personal with the redhead who had been with him on that never-to-be-forgotten weekend when she'd catered for his cousin and her husband.

Sick to her stomach, her emotions all over the place, she swallowed the contents of her glass in one go. The slinky redhead had been his latest squeeze that weekend. Now she was all over him, making a public spectacle of them both. Her face flamed. How dared he invite an ex-lover to his wedding? Or was he planning to reinstate her?

'Dance?'

Anna glanced up, about to refuse, saw Nick looking decidedly gloomy, and said, 'Why not?'

'I'm not much good at this,' he said, 'and proved it by treading on her foot.

'Not to worry.' Avoiding his size twelves would take

her mind off what Francesco was doing with that woman! 'We can just shuffle. Where's Melody?' The invitation had been for both of them.

'She couldn't make it. We were both gutted. We were looking forward to it, and to spending her weekend off here in London—booked a hotel and everything. Dammit—sorry!' he grumped, as he steered her into another couple. Holding her tighter, until she felt she would never be able to breathe again, he explained dourly, 'She's a vet nurse. There's only three in the practice. One's on holiday, and the one who was supposed to be on duty came down with a viral sickness, so poor old Mel had to fill in. So I'm on my tod.'

'Poor you!' Anna sympathised, glancing up and finding Francesco's eyes on her from the far side of the dance floor. He looked furious. No sign of the redhead. Furious because she was dancing with Nick?

Her heart skipped. He had given her ample evidence that he couldn't stand to see her old friend around her. And she'd accused him of being jealous. He'd denied it, of course, but you didn't feel possessive of someone who meant little to you, did you?

'I think I'll give the next dance a miss, Nick.'

She'd grab her brand-new husband and ask him why he'd been in a clinch to music with his one-time lover, inform him that if he thought he could resume his old womanising ways while he was married to her then he could darn well think again!

'Good idea,' Nick responded as he escorted her from the dance floor, heading for a pair of vacant gilded chairs, his arm around her narrow waist. 'Wait here.' His bluntly good-looking face was beaded with sweat. 'I'll fetch us a drink—something long and cold. I'm sweltering.'

The words to tell him not to bother on her account, because she was going to find Francesco, nail him down if necessary, died on her lips as he promptly disappeared in the direction of the bar. Shrugging slightly, she turned and found herself face to face with the redhead.

'I suppose I must give you my congratulations?'

'Thank you.' Anna didn't want to acknowledge the woman, but pride forced her to respond.

'Don't thank me.' The glossy scarlet lips parted on an insincere smile. 'Thank your own forward planning and fertility. Entrapment, I believe they call it.'

'I can't believe you just said that!' Anna was shaking inside with the force of her emotions. Was that how Francesco viewed his situation? Probably, she conceded in utter misery, and was drainingly humiliated when the other woman smoothed the dark green slinky fabric of her daringly low-cut dress over her snake hips and responded.

'No? Everybody thinks it—even though they're sweetness and light to your face. But that's not my style. Call a spade a spade, that's me. Francesco married you because you made sure you got yourself pregnant— why else would he tie himself to a bog-standard cook? But take it from one who knows. He won't be faithful. I got it from the horse's mouth. He invited me to your wedding specifically to tell me.'

CHAPTER THIRTEEN

As Nick appeared with two brimming glasses Francesco arrived, his eyes shooting ice as he said, cold as permafrost, 'My wife won't be needing that. We're leaving.'

The emotional upheaval going on inside her head meant Anna couldn't think straight, never mind resist, as a long-fingered hand clamped around her upper arm and hustled her out into the vast reception area.

He spoke into a mobile phone, clipped, authoritative, then snapped it closed and growled, 'Did you train him to dance attendance?'

'Don't be silly!'

'What was silly,' he countered, his eyes glittering, narrowed, 'was the moony love-lorn look on the guy's face as he trundled you around in a bear-hug—as if he couldn't face letting go of you.'

Looking up into his tension-riven features, Anna felt a reprehensible stab of triumph. He *was* jealous of Nick! That being so, could he really intend continuing his affair with that woman?

Or was it a case of sauce for the gander but not for the goose?

Firmly resisting the urge to string him along—and in the light of what the slinky redhead had said to her and the way they'd been practically seducing each other on the dance floor he deserved it—she informed him coolly, 'Nick was fed-up. Melody—the woman he's crazy about—couldn't be here. They'd planned to stay on for a day or two in London, but she'd had to cancel to cover for a sick colleague. And it wasn't a bear-hug! He was holding on to me because he kept on bumping me into other couples. He's got concrete boots when he's dancing. So don't lump me and Nick into the same league as you and *that woman*!'

'What's that supposed to mean?' Apparently unmollified by her defence of Nick, he was really on his high horse. His waiting silence was like an unscaleable brick wall, but Anna was too enraged to back away.

'The redheaded harpie you were practically seducing on the dance floor just accused me of entrapment and told me you'd invited her to our wedding to tell her that the fact that you were married wouldn't interfere with your affair with her. How sick is that?'

'Dio mio!' Francesco uttered grimly. Two hands on her upper arms, he swung her round to face him. 'That is pure poison!' Strain tightened his sensual mouth. 'I swear on our son's precious life that I have never had an affair with that woman. I hardly know her. She is my cousin's friend. Silvana invited her that weekend—she's a hopeless matchmaker, and the two of them obviously hoped something would come of our proximity.' He gave her a tiny shake, silver eyes searching emerald. 'I wasn't interested and I let her know it. I haven't given

another woman a single glance since I lost you—I refused to believe it, but I was still in love with you. I never stopped.'

'Oh!' Light-headed with happiness at that unexpect-edly emotional statement, Anna felt her eyes brim.

'She's just out to make trouble,' Francesco delivered fervently. 'It was she who was all over me, and apart from creating an undignified scene on my wedding day there was nothing I could do about it.' A muscle jerked at the side of his strong jaw. 'I can't ask you to trust me. I didn't do you the courtesy of trusting you, and for that I can never apologise enough. But we will confront the wretched woman, wring the truth from her.'

Hell hath no fury like a woman scorned! Those old sayings always hit the nail on the head.

Anna grinned. The man who was always right was actually saying sorry! 'There's no need for that,' she said with conviction. Her eyes were glowing. 'I trust you. You love Sholto. You would never have sworn to something that wasn't the absolute truth on his little life. And while we're about it—' she gave him a look of mock reproof '—you can stop being jealous of Nick. We've been good friends since we were barely out of nappies. Yes, he did ask me to marry him.'

She reached up to stroke the frown of displeasure that now drew his dark brows together. 'Because he was worried about me being a single parent. But, as I pointed out at the time, we weren't in love with each other, and, although I was touched by his offer, I wouldn't have been selfish enough to let him make such a sacrifice, because one day I knew he'd find someone he was crazy about. And now he has. In any case, I was still in love with you. Though, like you, I tried to deny it.'

That charismatic grin transformed his spectacular features as he briefly crushed her to him. 'You still love me?'

'Of course.' She tilted her head back. 'I tried to tell you before, but you wouldn't believe it.'

Francesco gave a driven groan. 'I have been a fool!' Gently, he stroked away a strand of blonde curls from her forehead. 'I will spend the rest of my life making it up to you, I promise, *amore mia*! And now we go!' He swept her up in his arms, the beaded skirts of her wedding dress trailing on the floor, and headed for the service area, past the kitchens and through a narrow door.

'What are you doing?' Not that she cared. Whatever he did was fine with her! Her arms looped around his neck, she didn't know how her body could contain such happiness. He *did* love her!

'Avoiding the photographers—the car is waiting.'

Arnold was waiting by the spacious Lexus, she registered, as Francesco's long stride hit the cobbles of the delivery access. 'Shouldn't we be seen off?' Common sense reasserted itself as her gorgeous husband slid her down his fantastic body. 'I promised to make sure Cristina caught my bouquet. Only…' Her brow creased. 'I've already lost it.'

'Shush.' Smiling lips stopped her words. 'The last I saw of her my niece was waltzing around the dance floor and her partner was your bouquet. I challenge anyone to take it off her! And I don't want to be "seen off", as you put it. I want out of here. Now. With you. We fly to Italy.'

Sholto was fast asleep in the car, securely fastened in his baby seat. Anna slid in beside him and Francesco followed, taking her hands as Arnold, grinning broadly, went round to the driver's seat and eased the big car smoothly away.

'I can't travel in a wedding dress.' Anna just loved the way he lifted her hands to his lips, placed tiny kisses in the palms, along the sensitive skin of her inner wrists.

'There's no law that says you shouldn't.'

'True.'

'I adore seeing you in a bridal gown. I adore having a bride—I will take it from you tonight.'

Such a wealth of promise in that statement of intent. A deliciously convulsive shudder shot through her. 'I can't wear it for the whole of our honeymoon,' she gasped, giggling.

'As our honeymoon will last for the rest of our lives, that would be impractical,' he conceded on a purr. 'Peggy has packed for you and Sholto. Anything missing can be easily rectified. I shall like taking my wife shopping. Spoiling her.'

As his private jet became airborne Francesco undid his seat belt and did the same for Anna. She looked flushed and happy, utterly adorable. His son was asleep in the skycot, his Italian housekeeper was expecting them, and the future promised everything he could hope for. And more.

'If this is entrapment then I'm all for it,' he told her softly, prepared for her immediate objection.

'I didn't deliberately—'

'I know you didn't, *cara mia*. Neither of us acted responsibly that first time. How could we? And I will give thanks for that for the rest of my life,' he stated with startling sincerity. 'If it hadn't been for our son we would never have found such happiness. So if this is a trap it is pure honey, and I gladly wallow in it.'

'Me too,' she sighed blissfully, nestling against him as he put an arm round her shoulder and shutting out the hideous thought that if she hadn't conceived she might have spent the rest of her life telling herself she hated and despised him. 'I'm not being picky, but when did you decide you could trust me? I know why you didn't—you were sort of programmed, I guess. But I would like to know.'

He shifted slightly, holding her eyes with his steady gaze. 'I was a mad fool. After the time we spent together on Ischia I truly believed I'd found true love and trust. Then your father asked me for a large amount of investment and I felt betrayed. Hurt beyond healing.' He dragged in a breath. 'I am so sorry for thinking for one moment that you were even remotely like my mother.'

'What happened to her?' Anna wasn't afraid to broach the taboo subject now. It was good to get him talking.

His face sobered. 'We heard of her death in a car crash with her latest rich lover shortly before Father died. He'd spent the intervening years pining for her, hoping that she'd eventually return to him and her children. When that hope was extinguished, my guess is he just gave up on living.'

As he'd given up on the children who had needed him years before that. 'So when did you start to trust me?' she pressed, to take his mind off such an unhappy track.

'When I started to think with my brain instead of my prejudices,' he confessed rawly. 'At first I put down your vehement refusal to take anything from me—in spite of my acceptance of responsibility for your and our child's welfare—to a plan to get far more from me. I should have been locked up!' he castigated herself bitterly. 'Then when Sholto was born, and I knew I had to be a proper father to my son, I asked you to marry me.'

'Told me!' she murmured, cuddling closer.

'You did not accept with the greedy happiness I was programmed to expect,' he responded drily, drawing her even closer. 'It was only on the night I put my crazy plan for a calm marriage to you in that restaurant that I finally found my sanity and started to put the pieces together. The way you'd refused to accept lavish maintenance payments before the birth; your reluctance to accept the clothes I paid for; the way you spurned the engagement ring I thrust on you which, to my knowledge, you had never worn. I had done you a great injustice. I loathed myself. I booked into a hotel and spent the most miserable hours of my life.

'To rub salt in the wound of my misplaced distrust, and to confirm what I already knew in my heart, I invited your father to meet me last night. It was just as you had said. You'd had no idea who I was or what I was worth. But he did—from reading the financial press. He told me he had never mentioned the episode to you—he was too ashamed of his crass behaviour. He explained that once he got an idea in his head everything else went right out of it. He hadn't thought he had jeopardised what we had between us. He hadn't realised our brief holiday romance—as he saw it—was serious. I can tell you he was totally gutted when I pointed out just what he had done.'

'Oh, goodness!' Anna heaved herself upright. 'Dad tried to tell me on the way to the church. But I told him to button his lip.' When he'd claimed it was his fault she'd thought he was talking about the gaggle of photographers! If only she'd listened to him she wouldn't have spent all that time agonising over whether Francesco had meant what he'd said when he'd told her he loved her at the start of the ceremony.

Her voice earnest, she pressed, 'No more misunderstandings. No more secrets. Promise?'

'Promise.' His voice was a purr of happiness as he lowered his dark head and kissed her.

The *palazzo* was something else—perched on a wooded spur, surrounded by sensationally beautiful gardens, the verdant Tuscan countryside rolled out beneath it.

'It's just perfect,' Anna breathed as Francesco, carrying Sholto, took her hand and led her in to meet Katerina, the housekeeper, and a group comprising daily helps and outdoor staff whose names she promptly forgot.

Beaming at them all, she promised herself she would take pains to remember their names in the future, would get to know them, learn to speak Italian. She stood by, deliriously happy, as Francesco presented the now wakeful wriggling baby to his staff.

The rest of the late afternoon was spent settling Sholto into his perfect nursery, happily arguing over who should bath him, finally doing it together and both getting their wedding finery liberally soaked. When the happy, replete baby lay fast asleep in his fancy crib, and they had agreed that not only was he perfect but completely remarkable, Francesco led her on a voyage of discovery around the magnificent property, her wedding gown trailing.

As they entered the grand salon, with its vaulted and elaborately painted ceiling, cool marble floor, priceless antiques, porcelain bowls of fragrant flowers everywhere and long windows open to the soft warm air, Anna breathed, 'Wow! You live in some style!'

'*We* live in style,' he stressed, his arm tightening around her waist. 'But, remember, if there is anything you want changing it shall be done.'

'Everything's just perfect.'

'I am glad!' His smile warmed her. 'The house and lands have been in my family for generations. Apparently, my mother hated it. She preferred bright lights, city living. This place was unvisited for long years. It became sad and neglected. When I inherited I made sure it was brought back to life.'

Anna melted inside. At last he was talking about the parent who had done him so much damage quite naturally, with no trace of bitterness, just stating facts. The damage was healing. There was one last thing she wanted to know.

Tilting her head to look up into his face, she asked, 'Tell me why—with all this luxury at your disposal— were you living in that stone shack when we met, dressing like a beach bum and wearing a pretend gold chain that left green marks on your skin?'

A wide grin slashed his features. 'Escapism. I love

the sea. I go there to unwind, to pretend I'm not a millionaire with a world-spanning business empire to run. I am incognito, living like a peasant, messing about in a small boat. I am not to be disturbed. But on the day we met one of my senior PAs had broken that rule, had come to me with a problem he believed only I could solve. As punishment I made him accompany me to drop lobster pots while he ran the problem by me! On our return to my private cove I found the most beautiful creature I'd ever seen. And we both know what happened then.'

'We fell in love,' Anna supplied softly. 'But why wear that tacky chain? Wasn't that overkill?' She reached up to draw his head down to hers, green eyes wickedly sparkling as his hands drifted down over her curvy hips.

He eased her forward against the hard cradle of his manhood in one smoothly erotic movement and answered, his breathing unsteady. 'Cristina gave it to me. My sister and her family were staying at my hotel for a couple of days. I had to wear it; she'd bought it with her pocket money. You'll recall I had to show some people around the island? Sophia and her family. You got the impression I was a freelance tour guide, picking up a few euros where I could. I didn't put you right. How could I when the last thing I wanted was for the lovely, sexy young woman I found to know who I was?'

Pressed against the urgency of his powerful body, Anna was melting, boneless, but she found the breath to assure him, 'I loved you when I thought you were a penniless drifter. If you lost everything tomorrow I would still love you, and—'

Claiming her mouth, he stopped her words with a hunger that sent her spinning into orbit, and she was so weak with wanton longing that she was a molten pool of submission as he swept her into strong arms and carried her out, mounting the curving staircase with determined strides, nudging open the opulent bedroom they were to share and setting her on her unsteady feet.

'My bride.' Long fingers deft, he began to undo the tiny buttons at the back of the wedding dress, and the hot ache inside her escalated to almost uncontainable proportions as the bodice fell away from her pouting, sensitised breasts. He smoothed the rest of the costly fabric from her hips, revealing tiny lacy panties, and groaned deep in his throat, telling her with husky intent, 'The moment I turned and saw you enter the church I promised myself I would do this.'

He scooped her up and laid her on the rich satin coverlet of the massive bed...